BETRAYED

JOAQUIN FUERTES MAFIA CARTEL

FUERTES MAFIA CARTEL

CHIQUITA DENNIE

LATEST RELEASES

Latest Releases from Chiquita Dennie

The Early Years-A Prequel Short Story

Antonio and Sabrina: Struck in Love 1, 2, 3,4,5

Heart of Stone, Book 1 (Emery & Jackson)

Heart Of Stone Book 1.5 Emery &Jackson A Valentine's Day Short

Janice and Carlo: Captivated By His Love

Heart of Stone, Book 2 (Jordan and Damon)

Temptation

Heart of Stone, Book 3 (Angela and Brent)

Cocky Catcher

Bossy Billionaire

Bottoms Up Heart of Stone, Book 3.5(Jessica and Joseph Short

Love Shorts: A Collection of Short Stories

Joaquin Fuertes (The Fuertes Cartel Book 1)

Exposed (Salvation Society Novel)

Joaquin Fuertes (The Fuertes Cartel Book 2)

Refuel (A Driven World Novel)

Pressure (A Driven World Novel)

Until Serena (HEA World Novel)
Antonio and Sabrina: Struck in Love 5
Heart of Stone, Book 4 (Jessica and Joseph)
She's All I Need
Red Light District (A Fantasy Romance Short)
Something Gained (A Romantic Comedy)
Aydin-TN Security Book 1
Upcoming Releases (2023/2024):
Dare To Love
The Carrington Cartel Book 1
Something Earned (A Romantic Comedy)
The Carrington Cartel Book 2

DISCLAIMER

This work of fiction contains strong language and explicit sexual content and is only intended for mature readers. This story may contain unconventional situations, language, and sexual encounters that may offend some readers. This book is for mature readers (18+).

DISCLAIMER

INTRODUCTION

Grab some wine and get ready for more spicy, sinful, sexy suspense.

Are you signed up for my newsletter?

Join today and find out all the latest in new releases, contests, giveaways, sneak peeks and more.

www.chiquitadennie.com

SYNOPSIS

Joaquin

I'd prepared myself to slow down and be a husband and father to my children now that our lives had blown up in public. Sofia was still working and traveling nonstop as an actress and singer. I'd tried not to let my frustrations show and spill over into my family or business, but deep down, I could feel her pulling away more and more. Being the boss of a cartel didn't mean anything to my wife because she fell in love with Joaquin and not the don of the Fuertes family.

SOFIA

"Three, two, one, action," the director blurted out. The camera started rolling, and lights shined down on the set. My eyes were fixed on the mirror as I composed myself before I turned and walked away. Shamar came into view as I tightened my robe.

"Kendrick, I've been your wife for the past five years. I refuse to let them win."

"Cut!" the director shouted.

While the makeup artist touched up my makeup, the cinematographer rolled the lens back to reveal the playback footage. Since Joaquin and I got married almost two years ago, my life had just expanded even more. My last album received multiple awards, and I had been offered a lot of work, which made me a household name now.

"Sofia, let's try it with you really pissed off. Your character was sacrificed."

"Okay, Angela."

"You need me to change up anything, Angela." Liam asked.

"No, you're doing fine, Shamar. The chemistry is there;

we need to see the emotions." Angela held the script up for us to look at the lines one more time. Potentially, the film could be turned into a series. An escort falls in love with a former president, based off a book titled *Mutual Agreement of a Former President*. It simply made sense to me to put myself in another light upon reading the book and pitching it to the production studios.

"Try it one more time from where you're standing," Angela explained, stepping over to the monitor and pointing at me.

"Action," she shouted.

I took a few minutes to breathe in deeply, closing my eyes and counting to three. Shaking my head, I turned away then back toward him as my eyes welled up.

I reached up and gripped his chin. "I refuse to let them win, Kendrick. You do what's necessary."

"Cut!" Angela stated, and the crew cheered and clapped their hands. I smiled and bowed, mouthing *thank you.* Shamar held his arms out for a hug, and I embraced him.

"Oscar worthy," Shamar said, and I giggled, pushing him away.

"Stop playing. You know it'll never happen." He chuck-led, nodded at Hugo, and followed me as we walked off the set and headed to my dressing room. Hugo was more than a bodyguard since we met and dealt with my kidnapping. I thought of him as a friend right along with Gael. Swinging the trailer door open, I stepped up to find Cassidy on the phone, and my babysitter Madelyn was taking care of my babies. As soon as I reached over, I grabbed my little girl Jianna from the bed and sat opposite JJ. The cartoons on his computer screen captivated him more than anything else. I was always impressed with his big brotherly skills and his protective nature toward his sister.

"How's the filming going?" Cassidy stood across from

the door, texting on her cell. Since becoming my new manager, she carried a more significant load in my life. Every day was something new, and I appreciated that she hadn't run off or sold us out, knowing what my husband did for a living.

"Going fine. Did you get the information for the photoshoot?" *Pregnancy Magazine* wanted to do a shoot with the kids and me, but so far, I hadn't built up the courage to tell Joaquin. We fought about keeping the kids hidden, but as an actress and singer, my fans expected to know more about my life. Lately, I'd post a photo with them blocked out, but they knew Joaquin was my husband even though I kept him off my page.

"I emailed everything over. How are you going to convince him?" Cassidy leaned over and tickled JJ's foot. He giggled and reached his arms out for her to pick him up, as Madelyn pulled his shirt down, covering his belly. My baby boy had his father's dark, piercing eyes, auburn hair, chestnut skin tone, and strong temper if he didn't get his way. Joaquin spoiled him, and I knew as the firstborn, he probably wanted him to follow in his footsteps. Something I meant to talk with him about once our schedules cleared up.

"I don't know, but I need to hurry up if they want me to do the shoot soon."

Jianna closed her eyes, and I lifted her across my shoulder to burp her as she slowly dozed off to sleep.

"They would like an answer by the end of the week, Sofia." Madelyn came back into the room with a plate of food. I placed Jianna down to sleep, rose, and kissed the top of JJ's head.

"I'll talk with him tonight. Let me go shower, so we can go."

"Ewww…" JJ clapped his hands together in excitement.

* * *

Four hours later, we arrived at our home outside the city that Joaquin had purchased years ago after the kidnapping. We were fully moved in, and the kids loved to be outside in the backyard to play. My parents could visit and not have to stay at a hotel since the place was big. Once Hugo parked the car, he headed around to the back passenger side to help Madelyn take Jianna out first, then JJ. I unbuckled my seat and opened the door, not waiting for his assistance, and he growled at me. I waved him off, not caring for the attitude.

"Hugo, you need to take a night off," I spoke, reaching for Jianna in her car seat. Rubbing my nose against her, I kissed her cheek. We all piled into the house, Madelyn set JJ down on the ground, and he took off running.

"He needs to be nice first," Cassidy mumbled under her breath. He held a harsh grimace on his face at her comment but decided to leave it alone. Neither one would speak up and say they liked the other, so I stayed out of the relationship. Joaquin never wanted to talk about his men dating, let alone his sister dating. Cassidy was family to us, and we were just as protective over her.

"Mrs. Fuertes, do you need anything before I start dinner for the kids?" The family chef walked out of the kitchen. I had a huge team of help, from Martha managing the housekeepers and the kids' schedule to Madelyn, my babysitter and assistant and Hugo, my bodyguard.

"No, it's just the family tonight. Is my husband home?" I removed my jacket and kicked off my shoes, rolling my sleeves up on my wrist.

"He's in his office," Martha replied, turning back toward the kitchen.

"I have some calls to make, and I'll get the notes from today sent over," Cassidy said, heading back out.

"You're not staying for dinner?" I asked.

She glanced at Hugo playing with JJ on the floor with Madelyn, and I smirked at him, ignoring her harsh glare.

"I had a huge lunch, still full."

"Yeah, right." She flipped me off, and I chortled, heading off to the back of the house toward Joaquin's office.

As I angled to listen in to the whispering on the other side of the door, a voice from behind me finally broke the silence.

"Ohh. I was just—"

"I forgot to tell you a seven a.m. call time tomorrow," Cassidy said. The door to Joaquin's office opened with Gael rushing out.

"What's wrong with him?" Cassidy inquired, and I shrugged.

"I'll see you in the morning." I didn't wait to be called into his office. I closed the door behind me, locking it from the inside and glancing briefly at Joaquin as he leaned back in his chair with his eyes closed.

"You get a good listen?" Joaquin asked.

"What are you talking about?" When he glanced at me, I pressed off the door and sauntered over to him, turning his chair around and plowing into his lap. Suddenly, he frowned at me, and I was taken aback by the change in his mood.

"You have to stop listening in on my meetings."

"I didn't listen in on your meeting." I pressed my palm against his cheek.

"How was work?" He changed the subject, placing his hands on each of my thighs.

"It is fine, work as normal."

"Hugo told me you had a scene with Shamar today, and you wore a robe." Joaquin's left brow rose.

"That's my job. It doesn't mean anything."

"A job you should be ready to retire from."

I tried to get off his lap, and he tightened his grip around my waist.

"Let me go."

"No."

"We've had this discussion before, and I'm not quitting."

"I have a job I need to go out and do. I need my wife to be home."

"What's the job?"

"Something you don't need to know about."

"Joaquin, that's not fair. We promised to not keep secrets."

"Sofia, enough. Where are my children?" He squeezed my thigh, and I smacked his hand away.

"What's wrong with Gael?"

"My sister is coming to dinner."

"You know they're dating, right?"

"Alessandra dates everyone."

"I want to do a photoshoot with the kids," I blurted out, and he stopped rubbing my thigh. I tried to reach for his hand, and he snatched it away.

"No."

"They're my kids too."

"I said no."

"This is ridiculous. You haven't given me a good reason. It's a closed set, and we're protected at all times."

"When is this shoot?"

"In two days."

"Move."

"No, I like sitting in your lap. Give me a kiss." I leaned

over to peck his lips, but he turned his head, and I ended up kissing his cheek.

I sighed and moved out of his lap to give him space.

"Stop pushing me."

"What are you afraid of, honey? You said we have triple the security now."

"That doesn't mean my enemies aren't looking for you."

"What if Gael came along with us?" I asked, praying he would let this one thing go.

He blew out a breath of frustration, rubbing his temples.

"No photoshoot, Sofia, and that's final." Joaquin turned toward me and pressed a kiss against my lips. Someone knocked on the door, and he answered, seeing JJ trying to come inside.

"My son, you look happy. Did you have fun with Mommy?" Joaquin was a natural with the kids, surprisingly. I never had to beg him to do anything or get up to feed or change a diaper. He loved being hands-on, and I was grateful to have that in a husband for times when I needed a break.

"Where's Jianna?" Joaquin questioned Madelyn.

"With Hugo in the living room," Madelyn replied.

Joaquin took the toy ball out of JJ's hand, watching him giggle in excitement as his father shook it in front of his face.

"I need to study my lines. I have an early call time tomorrow," I told him, strolling toward the door.

"Sofia."

"Yes." I stood with my back toward him.

"I love you."

"I know."

I drew in a deep breath, headed upstairs to our bedroom, and wiped the oncoming tears trying to fall.

Picking up my laptop, I checked my emails and social media. Clicking on the forwarded email by Cassidy, I read over the information for the photoshoot and replied to her that I wanted to go ahead with doing the shoot. Joaquin would just have to deal.

"Your phone is beeping."

I jumped in surprise and closed out the email, seeing Joaquin holding my phone.

"What's wrong with you?" he probed.

"Uhhh… nothing."

"I need to head out, but I'll be back for dinner."

"Where are you going?"

"Alessandra," he replied, and I knew something was wrong.

His sister was always in some type of drama, and since moving here permanently, his parents had put him in charge of keeping an eye on her.

"Be safe." When he bent down and pressed a kiss on my lips, he slid his tongue inside, and I dropped my computer on my side, wrapping my arms around his neck.

"Mmmm…" I sucked on his tongue, released him, then strolled out of the room as I watched the long strides of his broad shoulders as he texted on his phone.

I closed out of the group text, tossing the phone on the bed. No matter what, Joaquin would keep us under his wing at all times. I wasn't ashamed of who I'd married, and I refused to hide my children. Lifting the computer screen, I checked over my schedule and informed Cassidy to keep me updated on any changes. I then closed it out and put it on the desk. I twisted my wedding ring, walked out of the bedroom, and went to check on my babies in the playroom. I laughed when JJ focused so hard on Paw Patrol, and Jianna was in her baby chair, giggling at him. My life had expanded from having to handle what state I was singing in for the night to now chasing babies around a playroom.

"Who's hungry!" I clapped my hands together and tickled Jianna on her stomach.

"Hungry!" JJ excitedly jumped up and down.

"Me too. Come on, big boy." I grabbed his hand, picked Jianna up, and went to the kitchen. I helped them sit in their highchairs, and Martha passed me JJ's plate of veggies, cut-up chicken, and water. I picked up a bottle out of the fridge for Jianna and sat at the island to feed her while I listened to JJ talk our ears off. I chuckled at his animated expressions of what he loved and leaned over to wipe his hands clean of the food. I glanced up at the clock and noticed it was getting late. Dinner was almost done, and Joaquin once again wouldn't make it on time.

"I'm going to take her upstairs and get her ready for bed." I took the bottle out of Jianna's mouth and held her over my shoulder to pat her back.

"I'll keep a plate waiting for you."

"Thanks, Martha. He should be finished in another ten minutes." I rubbed JJ's head.

"No worries."

I kissed the top of his head and strolled upstairs to Jianna's bedroom, grabbed a fresh onesie, and took her to the bathroom. I watched her stare up at me with her father's features. Thirty minutes later, she was knocked out in her crib, and I went to check on JJ, asleep in his bed. I closed the door and checked the time on my watch. Still no Joaquin. I released a breath and sauntered to our bedroom to pin my hair up before setting a bath up to soak and fall asleep. He would be more than surprised when he noticed my schedule wouldn't be as available as he wanted. Mob boss or not, Joaquin needed a reminder of who he'd married.

JOAQUIN

The town car stopped in front of the club that was owned by people I didn't care to know, and I glanced out the window as Alessandra was escorted over to my car by my men. It was going on nine at night, and I'd promised Sofia I would be back for dinner, but that was to be determined if Alessandra continued to do stupid things. Gael was out handling another call. I thought it would be best not to get him involved, especially the way Alessandra was dressed. Lenny opened the passenger door, and she slid across the seat, wearing a dress that showed too much skin.

"I'm an adult, Joaquin!" Alessandra fussed.

"Shut up," I barked back.

"I'm telling Poppa!" she yelled, sniffing.

"You're going back to Italy."

"No!"

"The last thing I need to do is focus on my little sister getting drunk in clubs."

"Weren't you going at my age?"

"With protection. I knew not to drink around people I didn't know."

"All you care about is your work and nothing else," she complained. The car pulled out into traffic. That was the same argument Sofia was throwing at me, but I heard the opposite from my men because they felt I was losing focus on the cartel business. In addition, since I'd gotten married, Gael was responsible for many of the tasks.

"I'm dating Gael," she blurted out.

"He's my second in command; understand that if you get involved with him."

"He didn't want to date me because of you, but I convinced him you would be fine."

"Gael is much older than you."

"He doesn't treat me like a little girl."

"Stop acting like one by doing stupid things!" As I shouted angrily, my face became red.

"School takes up a lot of my time; it was just a night of drinks."

"If you can't handle yourself, I will have you shipped back to Italy."

"I can handle myself." With a roll of the eyes, she looked away.

"Tomorrow, I'm putting more guards on you."

"What! That's too much," Alessandra spat.

"Either you take the guards, or you come live with me."

"I'll take the guards."

She wiped the tears that welled up, and I hated to see my little sister cry, but she left me no choice as the oldest and her caregiver. I gave her money and paid for her apartment, thinking she would be on top of her classes, so I was shocked when I heard she was failing and partying more and more. If this was what I had to look forward to with Jianna,

I'd keep her locked in her bedroom until she was thirty. We arrived at the front of her condo, and I unlocked the door to step out. I checked the time on my cell and wiped a hand down my face. Alessandra leaned her head on my shoulder.

"You don't deserve her," Alessandra mumbled.

"No more alcohol; it makes you look foolish," I fussed, snatching her clutch and taking the keys out. I helped her through the doors and up to the elevator. Leaning her against the wall, I tapped on Sofia's name. The phone rang with no answer, and I cursed under my breath. I needed to make this right before we became even more fractured.

Ding!

"Come on," I told Alessandra and helped her inside the elevator. I hit the fifth floor and rode up, running all the thoughts of how Sofia would punish me for missing another dinner with our kids.

"I can make it from here, Joaquin." Alessandra held out her hand for her purse, and I walked around her, took the key out, and slid it in. I watched her stroll in and pass out on the couch.

"No more drinking. If I hear about this again, you won't like me." I bent down, helped to remove her shoes, and picked up the blanket off the couch to cover her up.

"I promise," Alessandra whispered.

Buzz! Buzz!

I glanced down at my vibrating phone and saw a text from Gael.

Gael: We have a problem.

Me: I'm handling something with Alessandra.

Gael: Is she all right?

Me: Drunk at a club.

Gael: She's trying to act like she isn't a part of the family.

Me: I'll remind her.

Gael: This can't wait.

Me: I'm leaving now.
Gael: It's not good.

* * *

APPROXIMATELY THIRTY MINUTES LATER, the car arrived at the address Gael texted to me, a small mom and pop shop, but there was something a little weird about it. As I walked to the door, Gael's men held the door open, and I stepped inside to look at the perfectly arranged food and drink display machines. A somber look came over Gabriel's face as he stood near the back door of the employee entrance. My attention was drawn to him as I waited for him to speak.

"You're not going to like this."

"What?"

"We have a new player."

My brow lifted in surprise. Everyone knew I ran the biggest gun ring in New York, on top of being the highest paid killer to get rid of any problem.

"Who?"

He motioned to the left of him, and I peered around him and saw a crate on the floor. I bent down to lift the top and saw a logo of a skull and foreign words that I recognized as French.

"Lusting," I mumbled.

"We need to see if more of those are around here."

"How did you know this was here? Who owns this place?"

I lifted the automatic weapon, checked the grip, and found the serial numbers were scraped off.

"One of our customers was approached with a proposal."

As I dropped the gun back in the crate, I stood and

looked around the room. It was a normal back office with a desk, TV, chair, and an exit door.

"Did they purchase it?"

"No, but he's interested in negotiations."

My left brow perked at that request.

"We don't give discounts."

"I told him that, and he'd like to speak with you directly."

"Everyone knows you handle all the negotiations."

"True, but if we want to keep this new problem from getting out of hand, we need to handle it now."

"Set up a meeting."

"You're giving him a discount." Gael trailed behind me from the backroom to the front door.

"Set up the meeting."

"Joaquin." He gave me a worried look.

Gael knew me better than anyone. I didn't let anyone steal from me or make my business look foolish.

"Call Alessandra tomorrow," I called out.

"No arguing?"

"She's an adult, but you know who I am and what I would do if something happened to her."

"I would give my life for her."

"Then we won't have any problems, but she needs to understand the people she's hanging with do her no good."

"I'm trying to not force anything."

"If she becomes a distraction for you or my life, I will send her back."

"I'll talk with her," Gael explained.

"Call me when that meeting is ready."

"What about our new friendly visitor?"

"Find out about Lusting."

"If they want in our area…"

I shut the door of the backseat.

"They dictate their futures."

"I thought you were stepping back on killing since the family has grown."

"Never underestimate a Fuertes."

Gael nodded and headed to his car. My driver pulled off down the road to head back home. I sighed and thought about the smile on my kid's face when I wake them up in the morning, and have our alone time together and able to give them my attention. Those two made everything else disappear, and I needed to remember to take in those moments before they grew older, and I missed out on precious time.

Past midnight, I walked through a quiet house, heading upstairs to peek in on JJ. I noticed him sleeping on his stomach like I used to do when I was younger. I closed the door quietly and checked on Jianna in her crib. Her little hands were balled up at her sides. I kissed her forehead and stepped away so as not to wake her, making sure the door was closed. As I strolled a few doors down the hallway, I approached our bedroom and released a long-held breath. I pushed the door open gently and stared up at my beautiful wife lying in bed asleep. I dropped my jacket on the chair, removed my clothes, and headed to the bathroom. I turned the shower on the hottest temperature, stepped in, and let the night wash away from me with my head down in thought. Fifteen minutes later, I grabbed a towel off the door and dried off. Sliding on my boxers, I turned the light off, climbed in bed, and pulled her naked body close to me.

"Mmmmm… you missed dinner," she muttered. I kissed her forehead. She slid her hand in my boxers and automatically, I got hard.

"It couldn't be helped…" I groaned when she squeezed my dick.

"What happened with Alessandra?" she asked, pulled my thick girth out of the boxers, and sat up to ease down on him.

"Shit!" I gripped her hips as she slowly rocked back and forth. Her low eyes exposed she was ready to take control.

Sofia stretched her arms out, lifted her hips, leaned down to take my lips, and guided her tongue to my mouth.

"Ughhh!" My hand firmly grasped her waist as I tightened my grip and pumped into her. She moaned as her head dropped back, her body quivering. We both fought for dominance in the relationship, and I hated when Sofia tried to question me. I smacked her on the ass, rotated us with me on top, and picked up the pace. She scratched my arms and chest as she cried out. She was close to climax.

"Joaquin! Right there!"

"Do as I ask, mi amore." Her hips bucked as her orgasm overwhelmed her. I released and fell on top of her, out of breath. She wrapped her arms around my back, and we fell asleep with me still inside of her.

JOAQUIN

I came downstairs fully dressed the next morning and noticed Martha only having my plate available for breakfast and coffee. She smiled and placed it in the usual spot of the island.

"Where's Sofia?"

"She's at the photoshoot, sir."

"I told her that was out of the question."

"I'm sorry, sir. She told me to pack the kids some food, and she'll have them eat at the location."

"Was Hugo with her?"

Martha nodded.

"I'm not hungry." I left the kitchen, stalked to my office in the back of the house, and slammed the door. I dialed Sofia's number.

"You've reached Sofia. I can't come to the phone right now. Leave a message."

"Sofia, call me back." I hung up and dialed again.

"You've reached Sofia, I can't come to the phone right now. Leave a message."

She knew I didn't want my children paraded around

the world and shown off. A man of my position needed to keep his family hidden, or at least my children. The sex we'd had last night I'd hoped would be a wakeup call to her, but something more was brewing between us that I didn't like.

Ring! Ring!

I answered the call.

"Sofia!"

"Joaquin, it's your father."

I sighed, not in the right frame of mind to talk with him about anything. I was slammed with thoughts of why Sofia had defied my orders and went on with the photoshoot.

"I'm here."

"How is your sister doing? We haven't heard from her lately."

"She's fine." I sat in my chair and clicked on the computer.

"I'm hearing differently."

"Then why are you calling me?"

"You seem distracted."

"I'm focused."

"Really? Because from what I see, you're losing a grip on everything."

"Define losing my grip." I clenched my teeth.

"I still have contacts in New York. I hear things."

"Are you trying to call to talk about your daughter or my business?"

"Unlike you, I have control over everything that belongs to me."

"I have control!" I shouted.

"For now. If your sister is getting drunk and showing up in these photos or on the internet, that's a problem for the family," he chastised.

I rubbed a hand down my forehead.

"I had a talk with her."

"Either you get a handle on things, or she comes back to Italy."

"She knows."

"And you'll lose my connection to guns if this continues."

"I can handle my own business."

"You're being watched."

"What do you know about Lusting?" I probed.

"Nothing."

"Gael found their guns being dropped in our area."

"A new dealer."

"Probably."

"You need to handle it."

"I will."

"Let me look into them first."

"A French design and wording."

"I'll send over what I find out."

"Thank you."

"And Joaquin."

"Yes."

"Understand your position."

I listened to the dial tone and held the phone out, then glanced at the family photo of Sofia and the kids. I'd been patient with her ever since the night of the kidnapping and wanted to keep her less caught up in my world, but she was taking her career to higher places and not thinking of the backfire it could have on our family or my business. I checked my business email and saw a few clients wanting me to take some jobs next week on short notice. I needed to think it over before agreeing even though the payment was one million. Anytime I spent away from my children out of the state was precious, minutes I couldn't get back or put a monetary value on. After I closed the email, I turned the computer off and walked to the wall photo of Sofia and pulled it open to reveal my safe. I grabbed a stack of money and a gun and locked it back up.

"Mr. Fuertes, do you need anything specific for dinner tonight?" Martha questioned.

"No, Martha. As a matter of fact, take the night off."

"Are you sure?"

"Positive."

"What should I say when Mrs. Fuertes calls?"

I stood at the open front door.

"Tell her you've confirmed things with me." I winked, shut the door behind me, placed my shades on, and walked to the awaiting limo.

"Anywhere specific, sir?" my driver asked.

"I need to go to Antonio's."

"Yes, sir, Mr. Fuertes."

He shut the door, and I buckled my seatbelt and dialed Sofia's number again.

"You've reached Sofia. I can't come to the phone right now. Leave a message."

Amherst pulled out of the driveway, and I held the cell up to stare at the third missed call from Sofia. This was only fueling the fire, making me want to send my men to bring her back home and lock her away with my children.

Buzz! Buzz!

Gael: Alessandra showed up for class.

Me: Good. I should be at Antonio's soon.

Gael: No updates on the Lusting situation.

Me: Meet me anyway.

Gael: Let me wrap up here.

After I sent a text back to him and said okay, Sofia finally replied back to my missed calls.

Sofia: I'm filming. What's going on?

Me: Where are my kids?

Sofia: They're fine, Joaquin. I wouldn't put my children in harm's way.

Me: We talked about this photoshoot not being a good idea.

Sofia: No, you demanded I don't do it.

The car stopped at a light. I watched the traffic ease through to the sounds of pissed-off people.

Me: We'll discuss this later tonight.

Sofia: Sex won't solve this issue.

Me: Alessandra held me up last night.

Sofia: That's not the only problem we're dealing with.

Me: I have a meeting I need to attend. I will talk to you later.

Sofia: Fine.

Me: Don't ignore my calls again.

Sofia: I was filming, and my phone was in my purse.

Me: I've stated what my concerns are.

Sofia: I'm being called to set.

The car arrived at Antonio's, and I closed out of the message thread, pushed the door open, and stepped out, looking at the surrounding areas. I went around the limo and shook hands with the guard on duty, and he opened the door for me. Looking around the closed restaurant, I noticed Carlo and Antonio sitting together at the back table near the window.

"Joaquin, how are you?" Carlo questioned.

I shook hands with Antonio, then Carlo, and grabbed the chair from the next table.

"I woke up with a lot on my mind."

Antonio picked up his glass of water and glanced at Carlo.

"Tell us," Carlo suggested.

"Do you know anything about Lusting?" I asked.

"Only thing I've heard about them was a few years ago. A gang out of France," Antonio recalled and slid his cup of water away.

"Why are you bringing this up?" Carlo asked.

"I might have a friend uninvited," I spoke in code.

"This Lusting," he quipped.

"Yes."

"We don't like visitors invited to the table." Antonio leaned forward clasped his hands together.

"Do we need to assist?"

"No, I've made a good reputation since I've been in America and New York City specifically. People know where I am."

"Are you still taking jobs?"

"Occasionally."

"How is married life?"

"Work." I smirked, and they chuckled at my statement.

"Give Sofia and the kids our best."

"Janice is constantly talking about a new trailer she saw Sofia in."

"Yeah, she's becoming a bigger star than before."

"I understand about having high profile women," Antonio said.

"Between her and my sister, my life is busy."

"So the ghost isn't ready for retirement?" Carlo pointed at the gun behind my jacket.

"He's always ready for action."

"Keep us updated, and we'll do our own checking on Lusting." Antonio looked at Carlo, and he nodded.

"What else do you need from us?" Carlo asked. Gael arrived, extended his hand to them, and sat next to me.

"Antonio, Carlo," Gael said, picking up the glass of water.

"I'm thinking of exploring new territory in Texas."

Gael took out his phone.

"I went out there a few months ago, after Joaquin talked

about how the borders are easily available to get guns in and out," Gael mentioned.

"You able to handle that type of increase?" On a napkin, Antonio scribbled.

"Depending on what the distribution is like, it could be lucrative," Gael replied.

"Keep me updated and contact this person to do research on the prospect." Antonio handed the napkin to me.

"Ezequiel Mota."

"Carlo and I have done business with him before. He's fair."

"I'll keep that in mind."

"Don't be a stranger. Even if your services aren't utilized by us, the girls want to get together," Carlo said, reaching out for a shake. I stood to leave.

"I'm always available for the De Luca Family."

"Again, keep us updated." Anthony tipped his glass into the air.

"Salute."

Upon leaving Antonio's, Gael and I walked to the car, and Amherst held the door open.

"Where to now?"

"Look into Ezequiel and Lusting. I want our reach to cover more shipment areas in case we need to expand beyond the loading docks for incoming deals."

"Expand that far? What if your father doesn't like your choice of business dealings?"

"He's not in charge."

"As long as you know," Gael replied.

"I need another favor."

"What is it?"

"I want to know everything about Sofia's filming."

"Joaquin, we've been through this before. She has her career."

"I know what she has. Her schedule is getting busier, and that's leaving very little time."

"I like Sofia for you, but you'll cause more problems with this request."

"Make the arrangements and see about a flight to Texas."

I climbed in and shut the door, waiting as the car pulled into traffic. The plan was to get back home early after a few more stops and spend time with my family for the rest of the day. Sofia would come home and expect me to be upset and angry, but my plan was to make sure the kids and her were welcomed with a nice dinner. Then we could spend alone time together once the kids went to bed.

SOFIA

The slow jams of the '80s played on the radio as the photographer came forward and took more shots of me holding Jianna's hand. JJ stood in front of me. All three of us matched in the same colors of cream, and red, to fit the background of me as a working actress and mother. We'd been here for over six hours, and I was enjoying myself, laughing, playing, and wanting to do even more. JJ became the star of the photoshoot, and they even mentioned him doing modeling for babies. That would never happen. Joaquin's calls were blowing up my phone, and I eventually had to text him back because Cassidy thought something could be wrong. I'd rather not deal with him being upset about me not returning any calls since the tension was already high with us. The filming project was going into extended shooting, and I needed to add more days on my schedule to do promo work and interviews, plus traveling would happen soon.

"We can break for lunch," the photographer said. We'd filmed together before in the past, and she knew how I liked to not fool around. Having a shoot at her studio in the Bronx was a little farther away from home, but we'd managed to stay on time and not run over.

"Thanks, Rosalie."

Madelyn came over and grabbed JJ's hand, and I sauntered with Jianna on my hip to the play area in the corner. JJ went to grab the toy truck, and I placed Jianna down on the patio and picked up a toy ball for her to take.

"How many more setups?" I asked Cassidy, took a seat in the chair next to the kids, and watched them play.

"Two more and only one of those with the kids."

"Do they need to change?"

"No, I think it'll be fine."

Cassidy passed me my phone.

"Any more texts from Joaquin?" I scrolled through my phone.

"No, and I think Hugo has sent photos or video back to him; it's been quiet since earlier."

"I doubt Hugo would do that, Cassidy."

"I don't put anything past him," Cassidy fussed.

Her upper lip pursed as she rolled her eyes at him.

"You two still haven't talked?"

"No reason to talk."

"You like him, and I think kissed him if I'm not mistaken."

"I was drunk." Cassidy grabbed the truck and bent down next to JJ.

"JJ, are you hungry?" I questioned, and he nodded.

"Yes, Mommy."

"Madelyn, can you grab some food from the bag in the corner please?"

I'd triple-packed for today and brought snacks they'd enjoy so I wouldn't have them on a sugar rush from the junk that was normally at photoshoots. Madelyn pulled out packets of apples, yogurt, crackers, and grapes for them to share.

"What are we doing after this?"

"We have a few video meetings, and then you're free for the rest of the day."

"Good, I'm exhausted."

"Just remember if we get the call to do the filming in Texas, you'll be away for a few weeks."

I blew out a breath.

"I know."

"Plus, you need to plan your next album."

"I can't think about that right now." I groaned, leaning back in the chair.

"Your career is at the top right now. I don't want to pressure you."

I wasn't upset about Cassidy going the extra mile to get me to the point in my career where I could decline certain roles. She'd taken the role of being a manager to a level that my previous management team never even imagined. I received so many offers and requests there was a possibility I'd be booked for the next two years, if I said yes to everything.

"I understand. Grab the opportunity while you can."

Cassidy stood, wiped her hands on her pants, and pulled the chair over to sit beside me.

"What do you think about doing a few appearances in Texas?"

"We're ready, Sofia!" Rosalie called out, changing the lights.

"Coming," I responded, rising out of the chair.

"Send me the details. I need to figure out what Joaquin is doing first."

"Great, give me a few minutes, and I'll send it over to your email."

Madelyn stood up with Jianna, and I grabbed JJ's hand to clean him up and help him stand to get set up for the next scene. Rosalie spoke on what she wanted for the final shoots with her team, and I listened in and helped to keep the kids hyped up and ready.

* * *

TWO HOURS LATER, we were piled in the limo together, and the kids were asleep in their car seats as the limo sped down the highway. It wasn't too late, and I had time to get the kids washed before bed and spend a little time together before I went over my scenes for tomorrow.

"It's so weird how much they look like Joaquin."

"My parents say the same thing."

"You just pooped out another version of him." Cassidy chuckled.

"When are you going to settle down?" I pointed out.

She waved away my question.

"Too busy."

"Life doesn't have to stop for you to have a love life and career."

"Honestly, I like focusing on your career rather than my love life."

I gazed over at Hugo in the passenger seat. I knew they had something going on and were secretly trying to keep it under wraps, but if he wanted something serious, and Cassidy didn't, this would drive a wedge between them even further.

"I appreciate the support, but remember you have a life outside of me and the kids."

"One day, I'll find someone," Cassidy muttered, looking out the window.

The car made it home and drove up to the front door.

Hugo got out to help the kids on the left side of the car, and I opened my door on the right and climbed out to pick up my bags. Madelyn carried Jianna's things. I removed my key and slid it in the front door, and there was complete silence as we walked through the corridor to the dining room. My eyes scanned around the room; it smelled like Pine Sol from a deep cleaning.

"I'll take them upstairs to get bathed," Madelyn said.

"Thanks, Madelyn. I'll get dinner started."

Hugo carried JJ in his arms behind Madelyn, and Cassidy followed to the kitchen. I strolled to my bedroom to change.

"Joaquin," I called out, nudging the door of our bedroom open, and it was empty.

I kicked off my shoes, removed the sweatpants and T-shirt, and grabbed my robe from the back of the door, along with a fresh shirt and pants. I pushed the bathroom door open and found candles were lit, with the lights low. I had no clue why. I stepped in farther and saw a note on the edge of the tub.

Relax, dinner will be ready in fifteen minutes .

I smiled, folded the note up, and put it inside my robe. I dropped it on the counter, slid in the tub of warm water, and placed my head on the back of the pillow so as not to get it wet. I let my body soak up the soothing aromas.

"Sofia! I'm leaving," I heard Cassidy yell from the other side of the door.

"Okay, call me later."

"Don't forget call time."

"I promise."

Thirty minutes later, I came downstairs, went to the kitchen, and saw Joaquin sitting with the kids, laughing together.

"Where is everybody?" I walked up to him and kissed

him on the lips. He gripped the back of my head and sucked on my tongue.

"I wanted to make dinner for you and the kids alone."

He sat between Jianna and JJ, and I pulled the chair out across from him.

"You want to tell me what that was earlier?"

I picked up the spoon to eat the risotto and veggies.

"We need to make sure we're not losing this time with the kids." He kissed the top of JJ's head.

"I don't disagree."

"How was the shoot?"

"It was good."

"I don't want my children in any more media photos."

"They're my kids too."

"Sofia, you can't expect to have the same life as before."

"I expect my husband to support my goals."

Jianna started to cry for me. I dropped the spoon, stood, and walked around the island to pick her up and bounce her to sleep in my arms.

"You went against my orders."

"I'm not Hugo or any other one of your men."

He whispered something in JJ's ear and helped him to finish eating.

"So you're ignoring me?"

"I'm going to get my son to bed. Then I plan on sleeping with my wife."

"Your wife."

Joaquin pressed a kiss to my cheek.

"Get the kids to bed."

"I have an early shoot tomorrow."

"Hugo will take you."

"I don't like your demeanor."

We walked the kids to their bedrooms.

"I have a lot of work to handle; fighting with my wife is not my goal."

"There is something else."

"Not tonight, Sofia." He pecked my lips.

I went into Jianna's room and took her to the bathroom to wipe her face and hands clean. I placed her in the crib and kissed her on the forehead. Turning the lights off, I headed to our bedroom, slipped out of my shoes, and pulled the covers back to lie down with the lights off. I fell asleep until his strong arms pulled me close to his chest, kissing the back of my neck.

* * *

TWO DAYS LATER.

I was on set, filming another scene with Shamar and waiting for them to call cut as we stood together in a tight embrace.

"Cut!" the director yelled.

"You brought it today, Sofia," Shamar said.

"Thanks, Shamar." The wardrobe department head brought over a robe to cover my dress. My character was going to dinner with his character. I picked up the water bottle, took a sip, and sat in my chair, watching the replay of the scene. We were becoming more and more comfortable bringing the story to life with each other. Cassidy pointed to the screen and noticed I picked up the fork in the wrong hand.

"We can do another take on that shot," the director said.

I sipped the water and listened to myself, checking to make sure that was the only mistake.

"That looks great," I muttered, pointing to us holding hands.

"We can do one more take of your side profile," the

director explained. I nodded, removed the robe, and stood as makeup and hair looked me over one more time. Escorting me back on stage, I released my hand and sat in the chair with the fake food and candlelight.

Shamar sat and joked to keep the fun flowing after a long day of filming.

"One more time, and it will be good for today." The director held the script in front of him on the table and pointed at the setup.

"Ready."

"Picking up from the beginning?" Shamar questioned.

I nodded and scooted closer to the table, picked up the fork.

"Action!" the director called out.

"Baby, I did this all for you." Shamar covered my hand on the table.

"I love how much you care." I smiled back and squeezed his hand.

Shamar leaned over the table and pecked me on the lips.

"Cut!"

Everybody clapped their hands for doing a great job on filming. Shamar helped me out from the table, and we gathered with the rest of the crew.

"Today was great, everyone. Remember we have filming coming up in Texas soon," the director commented.

"You guys have this in the bag for award season," Cassidy cheered.

"I'm just happy to be a part of the film," I responded.

"Are you ready to head out?" Cassidy asked.

I removed the jewelry and strolled off to my trailer with a team of guards as Cassidy talked about the details of our trip to Texas. I pushed open the door of my trailer and smiled at the kids playing with Madelyn. I kissed them both on the forehead and went to change my clothes.

Twenty minutes later, we arrived home exhausted from being gone the entire day once again. I allowed JJ to go to the playroom, and I saw Martha in the kitchen but no sign of Joaquin again.

"Madelyn, can you get the kids fed and ready for bed?"

"Of course."

"Thanks. I need to finalize some things with Cassidy."

Cassidy sauntered into the kitchen with her laptop and phone pressed to her ear.

"We can go to the living room."

She nodded, and I passed her a bottle of water and lifted an apple from the fruit bowl in the middle of the island.

"Where's Joaquin?" Cassidy questioned.

I sat next to her on the couch and shrugged.

"Who knows."

"If you need to reschedule our meeting, we can."

"It's fine."

"Okay, then we can start with a photo." Cassidy was cut off from a loud noise at the front door.

Bang! Bang!

"Move out of my way!" I heard loud familiar voices.

Startled, I put the cap back on the bottle of water, wondering who was yelling at the front door.

"Who is that?" Cassidy asked, and Hugo walked in with a tight grip on Alessandra.

"It's me… Alessandra," she whispered.

"What's wrong?"

"I need to talk to you."

"Can it wait?"

"Please, Sofia!"

"Give me a second," I replied and jumped up to escort her to Joaquin's office, away from the kids being disturbed.

"What?"

I shut the door behind us.

"I need your help."

"No." I tried to open the door and leave, but she pushed it back closed.

"Please, Sofia. I want to go to this party, and Joaquin's men won't let me out of their sight."

"Alessandra, you 're kidding, right?"

"No."

"I was relaxing after a long day of dealing with children and work. Your brother is missing in action."

"But I need you." She poked her lip out.

"No, you need to grow up and focus on why you came to New York."

"Haven't you wanted to be free of this mess and live life, Sofia?"

"That was before I got with your brother, and you know what I went through." I recalled the kidnapping and attempted rape.

Those early days of being with Joaquin should have come with a manual on dating a mobster. I thought I knew everything, but it was becoming clear that his world was more complicated by the day.

"It won't take long; you just slip in with me and leave after five minutes."

"What do you think Joaquin will say when he finds out I went to a club?" I opened the door and left with her behind me. I made it back to the living room with Cassidy and Hugo glaring at each other.

"He doesn't have to know. Besides, you need a girls' night out."

"No."

"I didn't take you for the submissive type."

I placed my hand on my hip, my lips pursed.

"That won't work on me."

"What are you talking about?"

"Trying to manipulate me into agreeing."

"You're right. I knew my brother was in charge, but I just figured you still had your way of handling him."

"Alessandra, I'm a grown woman; nobody is in charge of me."

"Then you'll go to the club with me." She held her hands up in prayer.

"Five minutes, and then we leave." I pointed at her.

"Yay! Yay!" Alessandra kissed me on the cheek and turned to leave the room.

"Don't make me regret this."

She crossed her middle and index finger and smirked.

SOFIA

I could already tell the night would be terrible soon as we came in and saw how the crowd was acting in the club. Alessandra had us in a section with some guys I'd never met before, but Hugo was close by and made sure we were watched. He didn't like that we'd come, but I promised we wouldn't stay long, and Cassidy was with me as well. The smoke filled the room, and I fanned it away and scooted closer to Cassidy as Alessandra smiled and picked up one of the champagne bottles to pour herself a drink.

"Do you think she knows those guys are expecting something for these drinks?"

"I told Joaquin something was up with Alessandra."

Walls thumped, and the DJ called over the mic for single women to come to the main floor.

"That's my song!" Alessandra jumped up, pulled her dress down, and reached for my hand.

"I'll be fine up here."

"Come on, Sofia. Have some fun." Alessandra extended her hand.

"No. I came with you, but I'm not dancing."

I was glad I'd listened to Cassidy and put my shades on so no one could recognize me.

"Ugh! Don't be boring at a nightclub." Alessandra stomped off down the stairs to the crowd. A hand was placed on my thigh, and I froze.

"Sexy, who are you with?" a drunken voice whispered in my ear.

"Please move your hand."

"You know you like it, sexy," he said.

"If you want to live, I suggest you move it before he does." I pointed at Hugo, whose eyes narrowed on the guy next to me.

He raised his hands in surrender.

"Cassidy, let's leave."

"Thought you'd never ask." Cassidy jumped up and extended her hand to me. I followed her out of the section, down the stairs, and through the crowds of people.

"*Ladies and gentlemen, we have Sofia Fuertes in the house!*" the DJ yelled.

I froze and turned to look over at the booth, and I saw Alessandra waving at us.

"Did she just do that?" I mumbled to myself.

"Where's Hugo?" Cassidy probed as camera phones were pushed in my face.

"Shit, we need to get out of here." I looked around the room.

"Can I have your autograph please?" a girl asked.

"Sorry, I'm not doing that."

"You're a stuck-up bitch!" she blurted out, and I felt a hand push me hard.

"What the fuck, bitch!" another woman shouted and shoved me in the shoulder.

"Sorry, this was an accident—"

Pop! Pop!

The entire club erupted in chaos. People shoved each other, fighting. I reached out to grab Cassidy's hand, and she was yanked down to the ground.

"Cassidy!"

Hugo fought a guy to get through to her, and before I could help her, my hand was yanked back, and my shades fell off.

"Let me go!" I shouted.

A tall figure of a man pushed me into the room, and I tried to get out, but he held his hands up in surrender.

"I'm not here to hurt you."

His accent was different, so I took a step back.

"Who are you?"

He smiled and reached his palm out. I looked down and back up to his narrowed dark, intense eyes. Even though it was nighttime, I could see he was a beautiful man at six-four, wearing a tailor-made suit.

"Emile."

Bang! Bang!

"Sofia! Sofia!" Cassidy yelled.

I strolled around him and opened the door. Hugo and Cassidy glared at the man behind me.

"Are you all right?"

"Yes. What about you?"

"Fine, but we need to leave."

"Where's Alessandra?"

"Who's this?" Hugo held his gun at the side of his body.

"He's okay, Hugo."

"What are you doing here with her?"

"Hugo, it's fine. He saved me."

"We don't have time, Hugo. We need to go."

Hugo tucked the gun back in his side, and I released a

breath and started toward the front entrance, but Hugo blocked me.

"The car is in the back," Hugo said.

"Joaquin is pissed," Cassidy whispered in my ear.

I looked over my shoulder and saw Emile staring back at me, and he winked. I climbed in the car, sitting next to Alessandra arguing on the phone with someone I could only assume was Gael. Hugo started the car and drove down the alleyway of the back entrance. I searched around for my purse and realized I didn't have it with me in the car.

"I lost my purse."

"Maybe tomorrow we can call to get it back." Cassidy pulled her phone out, scrolled, and showed her text thread of people mentioning a shootout at the club.

"This is a disaster." I groaned, leaning my head back on the seat.

"I'm not in the mood," Alessandra blurted out.

"What's going on with Alessandra?"

The car went silent as we rode on the freeway to our house.

"Sofia, you can't blame this on me." Alessandra placed her hand on her chest in shock.

"Actually, I can."

Alessandra rolled her eyes.

"You're just like my brother and Gael."

"Are you still going to school?"

I hadn't stayed on top of her lately with my schedule and the kids, but now, after the way she behaved in the club, she was doing more than just hanging with the wrong crowd.

"Yes, school is fine."

Hugo pulled up to the driveaway and parked, and the door was yanked open before he could turn it off.

"Hugo, make sure Alessandra gets home," Joaquin said in a low, even tone.

"Joaquin."

"Sofia, get in the house."

He turned and walked up the steps. I blew out a breath and followed him inside, nervous at how the night was only getting worse if we got into a shouting match.

"I'll call you tomorrow," I called out to Cassidy.

I shut the door behind me, and he set the alarm, slid his hands in pockets and leaned against the door.

"Let me explain."

"Who is the guy you're with?"

"I wasn't with anyone."

Joaquin cocked his head to the side and hiked his brow.

"Do you understand what you've done?"

After removing my heels, I went upstairs to our room, ignoring his questions.

"I'd appreciate you not condemning me for something I couldn't control." I turned the knob and dropped my shoes at the side of the door, removed my jewelry, and picked up the makeup wipes.

Joaquin stalked toward me and closed the distance between us. He gripped the bottom of my chin and put me in his line of sight.

"I won't ask again."

"All I know is that the shots went off, and we ran."

"Where was Hugo?"

"He was trying to get us out of the club, but somebody pushed him, and it turned into a fight."

"The man."

"Emile."

"Emile."

I sighed, dropped the wipes in the trash, and took my dress off, throwing it in the hamper near the bathroom.

"That's what he told me."

"You're not going out anymore."

"I'm a grown woman."

"My wife was almost killed. Do you know what message this will send to my enemies?"

"Is that the only thing you're worried about?"

I covered myself with his white shirt, stomped over to the bed, and climbed in, turning my back to him.

"Never question what I love more, Sofia."

"Could have fooled me." I wiped a tear that fell down my cheek.

"I think Alessandra needs to go back to Italy."

"She's obviously going through something."

"Get some sleep. We'll talk more tomorrow." He pressed a kiss to my cheek and started to leave.

"Where are you going?"

"I need to take care of some work. I'll be back."

"Don't take too long."

* * *

Two days later, I was preparing to do some pre-promo for the film with Shamar. Plus, the photoshoot with JJ and Jianna was trending, with people wanting us to do a reality show, which I'd never agree to do. I sipped on water through a straw Cassidy had brought over and waited for the camera crew to prepare for the interview.

"I think we have lifted off," Pamela, the reporter from Big News Media, said.

"Which one is this? Number fifteen?" Shamar joked, and I chuckled, feeling exhausted from sitting and moving from room to room, answering the same questions.

"That's the life of acting. We have to do promo," I replied.

"Ladies and gentlemen, I'm super excited to be sitting with you two," Pamela remarked.

"We're just as excited," Shamar said.

"Let's get started with the obvious question. How do you two feel about the story?" Pamela questioned.

Shamar motioned for me to answer first.

"I think we're both excited and relaxed, which makes the story come together on screen easier," I explained.

"From everyone I've talked to, this role was meant for you," Pamela said.

"That makes me feel good."

"So do you think you two will work together again?" Pamela asked.

I pointed at Shamar, and he laughed.

"I hope we get the chance; she's been the best screen partner."

"You're just as amazing," I teased him back.

"I can see you two work well together, Sofia. I think my audience and viewers would like to know how life is married to Joaquin Fuertes," Pamela probed.

The smile I had fell. I blinked fast, turning to find Cassidy, and she was around.

"Excuse me."

"Your husband. Joaquin Fuertes is a mob boss, correct?"

"I think we shouldn't be talking about my personal life."

"Your personal life is on social media; I mean, you've recently done a photoshoot with your kids." Pamela clasped her hands together and stared at me.

"I know from being on set, they're lovely kids," Shamar brought up.

"But your husband is involved in illegal activities, correct?" Pamela asked again, and I didn't want to be unprofessional and show that she'd gotten the best of me. They were known to do gossipy stories on me constantly.

"Pamela is here to talk about Sofia as an actress," Cassidy approached, and I felt relief.

"If you're asking the audience to believe you're a clean-cut family, I think you're doing a disservice to our readers," Pamela commented.

"We're done," I said.

"I mean, you were trending from being at a shootout at a club. Was that because of your husband?" Pamela blurted out, and I almost lunged at her and choked her on camera. That would have just put me in a worse position with the studio and industry peers. I walked out of the room and back into the hotel room the studio rented for us to get dressed. I grabbed my purse and keys to get ready to leave.

"That was a setup."

"I know." Cassidy typed on her cell phone.

"Who are you calling?"

"Getting the studio to pull Big News from the press."

"She said the shootout was trending on social media."

"We should put a statement out."

"Was anybody hurt?" I asked.

"Not that I know of." She glanced at Hugo.

"Why do I feel like this is going to get worse?"

"What do you need me to do?" Shamar knocked on the door and peeked his head inside.

"Sorry about this, Shamar. I can't believe she tried to do this right now."

"Don't worry about it. I'm used to the gossip blogs." Shamar placed his hand on my shoulder.

"Thanks."

"I'll see you back on set." Shamar reached over and gave me a hug.

"Well, we might have a bigger problem than I thought."

"What?"

Cassidy passed her phone to me, and I saw a black and white photo of me and Joaquin in bed together.

"What the fuck!" I scrolled through two more photos of me naked with Joaquin having sex.

"You need to call Joaquin." Cassidy paced back and forth.

"Who is doing this?"

JOAQUIN

Standing in the room surrounded by some of my men, I listened to them run down all the information they could come up with on Lusting's character and the shootout at the club Sofia had gone to the other night. My sister was in class because I made sure guards were standing outside the room if she tried to leave. Sofia could feel sorry for her and want to be caring and supportive, but I was done with allowing Alessandra a pass.

"Gael, what do you have?" I questioned, scanning the office and watching the nervous looks on each man who came up short and expected to walk out of here alive.

"From talking with Alessandra, it was two guys arguing."

"Just random men arguing."

"She wasn't close to them, but I suspect it was a setup."

"They knew Sofia was inside."

"Probably followed her and Alessandra for a while."

"Anything on the video footage?" I looked at Steven, our tech guy.

"I ran video stills of everyone who entered the club and left; facial recognition came up."

"What is it?"

Steven turned the computer around, displaying the semi-blurry photo of a tall man with a low-cut buzz, thin nose, and broad shoulders.

"Emile Lusting," I muttered.

"The leader of the French mafia. They've been around for over thirty years," Steven read off the screen.

"Why is he here?"

"He's looking to take over."

"So he tries to go after my wife?"

"I think we need to make contact," Gael suggested.

"Now isn't the time to go to war," one of my soldiers commented.

"That's only the tip of my thoughts."

"He wants to push us out, correct?"

"Joaquin, if we do this and are still trying to expand to Texas, we need to make sure our bases are covered." I listened to Gael explain the details of our deals. My phone vibrated, and I glanced down to see a message with Sofia's name across the top. I typed in my password and pulled the message up. My eyes widened in surprise. I heard the cells go off my other men, and I looked around at their shocked eyes.

"It's him."

"Joaquin, we need to figure out what he wants."

"I know what he wants, and he's going to get exactly what he's asking for."

I gripped the phone tighter and went to dial Sofia and find out where she was, when her soft whimpers came through the phone.

"Why are they doing this to me?" Sofia murmured.

"I'm going to get to the bottom of this."

"Steven, get these photos taken down," Gael demanded.

"On it already."

"Where are you?" I started to walk out of the room.

"Locked in the bedroom."

"My babies."

"With Madelyn."

"I won't let this come back on you."

"This about you?" she probed.

"I won't like it; I think it's a message."

"Are you serious, Joaquin?"

"Mi amore."

"No, don't even think about trying to manipulate me."

"Sofia."

The phone went dead, and I growled and punched the wall.

"Take me to the club."

"We need to be smart about running into the club until we know for sure where Emile is located."

"I don't give a fuck who he is; he came after my family."

We climbed in the car, and I slammed the door and tried to dial Sofia back, but she didn't answer. I called Hugo to make sure he was with her at the house.

"Boss."

"Where is Sofia?"

"In her room, sir."

"My children?"

"Right in front of me."

"Put the house on lockdown; no one in or out."

"What's going on?"

"Lusting, a new enemy, has given the first shot."

"The photos."

"And the shootout at the club."

"What does he want?"

"What they all want. My attention."

"Sofia's supposed to go back to work and fly out of town."

"Out of town where?"

"Texas."

My body heated up, and I became enraged at her not telling me about some work trip that she knew I wouldn't approve of. I promised myself I would never be caught looking weak by giving someone the opportunity to get into my home and near my children.

"She's not going anywhere."

The car arrived at the club, and I had two SUVs deep with more guards. I finished telling Hugo I would be home soon.

"Mr. Fuertes, can I help you?" the security guard asked.

"Where's Emile?"

"Who?"

I passed my phone to Gael and turned my head. Smirking, I punched him in the stomach, and he fell to the ground.

"Arghhh!"

Another guard came out shouting, and I lunged, gripping him around the collar of his shirt and pushing him up against the wall. I pulled out my knife and held it against his throat.

"Tell Emile Lusting his guest has arrived."

The guard held his hands up in surrender and nodded. I released my tight grip and let him lead me into the club. The bartender paused what he was doing, stared at the group of men holding guns, and blocked the door, motioning for the waitress to move toward the bar.

"Where is he?"

"In the back."

I shoved him to move forward and lead us to the back

room. As they walked down the hallway, he came upon more guards standing stoically at the door.

"Don't be a hero." Joaquin pushed the knife closer to his throat.

"Emile wants to see him."

The guard nodded, twisted the knob, and pushed the door open. I shoved his man forward and strolled in to see Emile sitting in his chair, smoking a cigar.

"Mr. Fuertes," he said in a deep French accent.

"What do you want?"

"Would you like a drink?"

"Gael."

Gael raised his gun and shot the guard in the leg.

"No need for the anger."

"How did you get in my house?"

"I wouldn't know what you're talking about."

"Do you know who you're making an enemy out of?"

He put the cigar out, stood from the seat, and came around the desk.

"Mr. Fuertes, I'm no harm to you or your family."

"How did you get in my home?"

Emile smirked, rubbing his chin.

"I apologize for being overboard."

I gripped the knife tight at my side.

"You don't want to do that, Mr. Fuertes."

"Why not?"

"My men have your home surrounded."

I glanced at Gael, and he lifted his phone to dial Hugo.

"Gael, I'm a little busy." Hugo sounded annoyed, rustling through the phone.

"Check outside," Gael demanded.

My eyes never left Emile.

"Why?"

"Just do it!" Gael shouted.

"Hold on, JJ," Hugo said.

"You see anything?" Gael asked.

"No, our men are patrolling," Hugo answered.

"Keep an eye out." Gael ended the call.

"We like to be undetected. The same way we got in, we can do it again." Emile grinned.

"What do you want?" Gael asked.

"I'd like to do business with you."

"Threatening my family doesn't prove to me I should work with you."

"I only ask, but we can do things the hard way," Lusting said. I raised the knife up and slid it back in my space place.

"Working together will never happen. I'm warning you now, don't threaten my family again."

"Sorry we couldn't do business together, Mr. Fuertes." Lusting extended his hand to shake.

I turned my back, stalked out of his office, and left the club. A few seconds later, Gael pulled me back before we got in the car.

"Your quietness is going to be called into question."

"He thinks he has the upper hand, but we're going to give him what he wants."

"Are you giving up territory?"

"We're giving him an early death."

Ring! Ring!

I picked up my ringing phone and saw Cassidy's name scrolled across.

"Why is she calling me? I just talked to Sofia."

"Maybe Emile did something," Gael answered, and we climbed in the car.

"Cassidy?"

"Mr. Fuertes, I'm with Sofia."

"What happened? We just spoke to her a second ago."

"It's your sister."

"Alessandra." I looked over at Gael, and he pulled out his phone and tried to dial Alessandra.

"I guess you haven't heard about her hanging out with the wrong crowd."

"I know, and Gael is going to speak with her."

"The club shooting is all over the Internet and now the photos of you and Sofia."

"Where is Sofia?"

"She's upset, but I wanted to see if you'd agree to a statement."

"Statement."

"A joint statement about the photos."

"No."

"But—"

"Cassidy, one thing you should understand is that I don't let things or people dictate my life."

"Yes, sir."

"Put Sofia on the phone."

"Here she is."

"Sofia."

I heard sniffing.

"I'm on my way home."

"Who is trying to ruin my career to get to you?"

"I have something in the works."

"Do you know they have me plastered all over the world, apparently in a sex tape of us."

I closed my eyes for a moment.

"He's being taken care of as we speak."

"I want this finished, Joaquin."

"I promise. Ti amore."

ALESSANDRA

$\mathcal{M}$any people would say I was spoiled because I wanted to be free and away from my parents. I grew up in Italy and Spain under strict rules, having my life dictated from the time I was born. Yes, I liked to party and drink with friends, but I worked hard and went to school to get my degree in fashion. *Have I done a few things that I shouldn't have done?* What twenty-two-year-old hasn't? My brother made a bigger deal out of things than it needed to be. On top of that, my boyfriend and his right-hand man Gael were acting more like him, being over-protective since we'd decided to become a couple.

I stepped out of the bathroom from a long shower with a towel wrapped around my waist and stopped at the sight of Gael sitting on the edge of my bed. I smiled and extended my arms out and approached him, but he nudged me away.

"What's wrong?"

"I should ask you that question."

I rolled my eyes.

"If you're here to yell at me, then you can leave." I placed my hands on my hips.

"Who are you?"

"I'm having fun. Is that a crime?"

"You got mixed up in a shootout with your brother's wife!"

"That wasn't my fault."

"What about you being out with some guy, and he's groping you?"

I forgot about the party I went to with some friends from school. A few guys approached us, and we got to talking and drinking. I told them I had a boyfriend, but there wasn't any harm in dancing with a few friends.

"It was harmless flirting."

Gael jumped up in my face, squinting his eyes.

"We're done."

"Wait… What?"

"You disrespect me, Alessandra. I knew this was a mistake from the beginning."

"Gael, you're making a bigger deal than it really is. Besides, I've never cheated on you."

"You need to live life and explore. I'm obviously not a priority, and I wouldn't want to hold you back."

"That's not true."

"Si, it is, mi amore."

"Did Joaquin tell you to do this?"

"Joaquin doesn't even know I'm here."

I grabbed a pair of high-waisted jean shorts and a crop top from the closet and got dressed.

"I'll listen."

"That's not the only problem."

"What else? I'm doing fine in school."

He tilted his head to the side, and I rolled my eyes.

"All right, I was late a few times and missed an exam."

"Do you love me?"

My hands were on his chest.

"More than anything."

"Then we should take a little break, and you should explore on your own."

"No!" I shoved him back.

"Alessandra!"

I cursed him out in Italian, and he ran a hand down his face and walked off, leaving me behind his back to push and shove to get his attention.

"Please don't do this." I grasped his arm.

"Let me go."

"Who is she? Did you cheat on me? You've hated the age difference."

"The only issue in this relationship is you." Gael opened the front door, and I stood in shock, released his arm, and watched him walk out of my condo.

"Arghhh!" I dropped to my knees in tears at not seeing Gael anymore. All my life, I'd loved him and wanted us to be together. Now, by my own doing, we'd broken up.

Ring! Ring!

"Hello."

"Alessandra? Are you all right?"

I looked around my home in disbelief that Gael wouldn't come back to me.

"No."

"Well, come out with us to the bar." My classmate Odessa was in her last year of design school and popular on campus. She was tall and blond with brown eyes, thin with a model body that had all the guys in love.

"I don't think it's a good idea."

"Why? This will be fun. I already have Rich and Eliot eating out of my hands," Odessa said.

"I just broke up with my boyfriend." I sniffed over the phone.

"All the more reason to let your hair down."

"I can't."

She groaned through the phone.

"Listen, you sound depressed, and I think you should come out. Get some fresh air."

Thinking over her words, I decided I could use a moment away from any memories of Gael and me together.

"One drink, and then I'm leaving."

"One drink," Odessa repeated.

* * *

THE ROOM WAS loud with blaring music, and I was on my third drink, sulking in pain from calling Gael for the third time in a row. My calls went straight to voicemail. I was tempted to go to his house, force him to speak to me, and then cook his favorite meals.

"To the single life!" Odessa held a glass in the air.

I froze when an arm wrapped around my waist, and a husky voice whispered in my ear, "Aren't you Alessandra Fuertes?"

"My friend just broke up with her boyfriend, can you show her a good time?" Odessa winked her left brow and giggled, falling in the arms of the guy's friend.

"He's a fool for hurting you," he said. I ignored him and waved for the bartender to give me another shot of tequila.

"Rich, take her on the dance floor."

"Not in the mood to dance."

"Come on, Alessandra. I won't bite… unless you need a little pain," he growled in my ear.

"Alessandra, if you're going to be bored, you could have

stayed home," Odessa blurted out. I nodded and figured it was time to get out of my funk.

"One dance."

"One dance, and then we can have a little party alone." He dug in his pocket and pulled out a bag of pills.

"I don't do drugs."

"Not drugs, just something to make you feel good." Rich opened the bag, pulled a pill out, and popped it in his mouth. Then he gripped my chin, pressed a kiss to my lips, and sucked on my tongue. I felt the pill ease into my mouth.

"Sexy," Rich said, pecking me on the lips. The music changed, and the crowd grew louder. I felt lighter on my feet and smiled.

"What was that?" I asked, swaying my hips. Odessa came up beside us and bumped into me. We laughed.

"Relax, Alessandra, it's fun and harmless."

An hour later, we were inside a diner with a group of six of us, drinking and laughing after hanging out at the bar. My mouth was dry, and I was hot and sweaty from dancing too much. It was going on one in the morning.

"What are you getting, Alessandra?" Odessa asked.

My eyes were low. I could barely keep my head up, and I thought I was seeing two Odessas.

"Huh?"

"Are you all right?"

"I don't feel good."

I fanned myself.

"You need some food in your stomach."

I shook my head.

"Can you call Sofia?"

"Who is Sofia?" Rich questioned, rubbing on my thigh. I pushed his hand away, crossed my legs, and slid my hand in my purse to grab my phone.

"I need to call my brother." I tried to dial Sofia's number when my head got drowsy. Someone yanked the phone out of my hand, and everything went dark. My eyes rolled in the back of my head.

My head was heavy, and I groaned and rubbed my forehead from the massive headache. When I opened my eyes, I saw I wasn't at home.

"She's woken up," I heard a voice say.

"Mhmmmmm..." I moaned.

"Alessandra."

"Sofia."

"Call the nurse," she said.

I looked around the room and saw Gael standing at the window with a hard glare on his face and Joaquin sitting in the chair near my bed. Sofia talked with a nurse, and I realized I was in a hospital bed, wearing a white gown.

"What happened?"

"You were drugged."

"Huh?"

"You're going back home," Joaquin said.

"Joaquin, not now," Sofia snapped.

"No."

"Either you go back home, or you're moving in with us," Joaquin demanded.

"I'm not a child!" I spat, and my head pounded.

"Then act like an adult. You could have been attacked or worse!" Joaquin shouted.

"Joaquin, can I talk to her alone please?"

"Odessa's my friend," I replied.

Gael shoved off the wall, shook his head, and sauntered to the door.

"Gael... wait," I called his name, trying to sit up.

"Don't. I'll check in on you later." Gael opened the door and walked out.

"Alessandra, that girl is not your friend," Sofia remarked, walked over, and grasped my hand.

"I'll be outside," Joaquin said.

"They hate me," I muttered.

"No, they're disappointed, and we have a lot going on."

"Don't let them send me back."

"You should think about what you're doing; it's interrupting our lives," Sofia argued.

"You're just like him, trying to run my life," I fussed, yanking my hand away.

"Anytime we get a phone call in the middle of the night with the words drug overdose, what do you expect us to do?" Sofia questioned.

"Can you leave me alone please?"

"Tonight, you sleep, but you need to make a decision. Tomorrow, you're not going back to your condo." Sofia kissed me on the forehead, and I closed my eyes and let the thoughts of Gael consume me as I drifted off to sleep.

CASSIDY

The next day.

The door of my bedroom squeaked open, and I wanted to yell at him for not answering my call again. I liked when he got pissed off. I bit my bottom lip, scooted up in the bed, and let the sheet fall from my naked body. His eyes turned animalistic, ready to attack his prey, and even though our night was cut short with everything happening with Sofia and Joaquin, I wanted to make up for the loss with him between my legs. Many people would say I was crazy for even thinking about dating a mobster, but becoming his fiancée was entirely another story. The biggest reason for our fights lately was me hiding our relationship. My job was to keep all eyes on Sofia and secretly, I feared dealing with the same problems that she was going through now.

"Breakfast in bed." Hugo kissed me on the forehead and placed the tray in front of me.

The food looked delicious, and I was starving for something to eat. When Sofia called me last night about

Alessandra, my main goal was to make sure the family was good and worrying about Hugo's safety.

"You don't cook."

"Delivery."

"Have some. I can't eat all of this by myself."

"I like to watch you eat." Hugo reached over and rubbed my nipple.

"Mmmmm…"

"Eat."

"I'll eat afterwards. I want something else." I pointed to his boxers, and he chuckled.

"No time for that. I need to get over to the house with Sofia and Joaquin."

"How is Alessandra?" I cut into the pancakes and fed it to him.

"Quiet, playing the silent treatment with her brother."

"She thinks Joaquin is going to send her back?"

"He already made the call."

"Just like that?"

Hugo slid out of bed, and I admired his wide shoulders and muscular back with tattoos of his family and friends.

"Joaquin has enemies, and Alessandra is being foolish."

"She's young like me."

"But you're not acting dumb."

"Well, only for you."

He winked at me.

"I want to come."

"No, you need to stay here out of trouble."

"I can help."

"Cassi." He called me by a nickname whenever he was serious about something. I poked my lip out, moved the tray to the side, and crawled close to the edge of the bed. He stopped and narrowed his eyes at me.

"Sofia needs my help just as much as Alessandra."

"You're going to tell her about our ring."

He pointed at the jewelry box sitting in the nightstand.

"It's too early, Hugo," I whined.

"I'm not your little secret, Cassi."

"When have I ever made you feel like you're a secret?" I rose out of the bed, closed the distance between us, and wrapped my arms around his waist. Hugo sighed, extended his arms to my lower back, and cuffed my butt cheeks. He peppered my shoulder with kisses, and I groaned, wanting to feel his thick shaft.

"Busy first," Hugo muttered and pressed a kiss to my lips.

I dropped my hands from around his waist, stomped to the bathroom, and slammed the door.

"Withholding sex from me won't work!" I shouted from the other side of the bathroom.

"Cassi."

"What!"

"Wear your ring."

The feeling of making it known to the world that I was getting married to someone my parents had only met a few times, that I half-lied about his occupation being a businessman. If they knew he was a trained killer, I'd probably be shipped out to a convent.

* * *

LATER IN THE AFTERNOON, I arrived at Sofia and Joaquin's home to a barrage of cars and men outside like it was Fort Knox. Once Hugo left earlier, I had some work to do, getting Sofia back on set and approved for flying to Texas for an upcoming film shoot. I parked my car, grabbed my laptop and purse, and knocked on the front door.

"Hi, Cassidy," Martha answered and stepped to the side, allowing me to enter.

I removed my glasses and followed Sofia's voice in the living room.

"How is she?"

"Which one?"

"Both, I guess."

"Alessandra is sulking in her bedroom, and Sofia is in the living room with the kids," Martha explained.

"Thanks."

When Pamela threw that question, I was pissed and ready to kick her ass, but I had to maintain my composure, or we'd be in more trouble. I stepped in the living room and chuckled at JJ trying to keep his food away from Jianna. That little girl was still in the body-feeding stage and thought she was grown and could have solid foods.

"He's so big." I ran my palm through his black, curly hair. He took after his father so much, even with that crinkle in the middle of his forehead that popped up when he was angry.

"Remind me to lock him and my sister up so they can't grow up any more."

Sofia stood and reached out for a hug. I rubbed her back and took a seat next to her on the couch.

"Where is everybody?"

"Joaquin is in his office with Hugo and Gael."

"Alessandra."

"Upstairs, refusing to come out."

"When is she leaving to go back home?"

"I think tomorrow."

"How are you handling all this?"

Sofia waved her hand in the air.

"I worked hard to have a career without any scandals, and now all that is being washed away."

"You can't think like that."

"Easy for you to say."

"What does that mean?"

"Nothing."

"No, tell me."

"Hugo."

"What about Hugo?"

"You see what I'm going through with Joaquin. Why would you do the same thing?" she whispered.

I opened, then closed my mouth in surprise that she knew we were an item.

"You two are more obvious than you think."

"I thought I was hiding it well."

"No, you're not."

"He wants to tell everybody."

"What do you want?"

"Honestly?"

"Yes."

"Don't take this the wrong way."

"Depends."

"I can't worry what happens to him every minute and if people are trying to kill him by going through me."

"Like my life."

I nodded, hating to have these thoughts.

"It's not easy. Sometimes I wish I could go back."

"Any other surprises pop up?"

"The studio called me."

"Huh… Why? I'm your manager."

"They're thinking of recasting my part."

"What!" I jumped off the couch, startling the kids. Sofia grasped my arm and yanked me back down.

"Sshhh."

"They can't do that. We have a contract."

"I know, and I threatened to sue if they tried."

"What did they say?"

"Talked about the bad publicity with my marriage and shootout."

"That's bull crap." I had to catch myself when JJ treaded over to me with his toy car.

"Baby, go finish your food," Sofia said.

"Are you still going to Texas?"

"Joaquin said something about us needing to be on lockdown, but I have no choice but to go for work or lose out on this opportunity."

"I think you should go. We can get extra protection."

Buzz! Buzz!

"Who is that?" I questioned.

"My notifications have been going off all day."

"I'm sorry this is happening to you. I tried to get a statement out, but Joaquin—"

"Stubborn, I know. Today, I was planning on talking to him about some things we need to change."

"If he plans on staying married to me, he's going to make some changes."

"Are you thinking about divorcing him?"

"Divorce!" Alessandra shouted.

Sofia rolled her eyes, and I groaned, turned at her disheveled attire of gray sweatpants and large white T-shirts with her hair unkempt. This wasn't the normal Alessandra we were used to seeing. The bags under her eyes told a story she wanted to hide.

"You're married to the Fuertes family; we don't believe in divorce," Alessandra preached.

"Alessandra." I tried to calm her down.

She shoved her hand in my face, and I could tell Sofia was embarrassed about her sister-in-law.

"Alessandra, my marriage is none of your concern. You've done enough," Sofia replied.

"Does Joaquin know you're trying to divorce him? Take his bambina and son away." Alessandra pointed at the kids.

"What's with all the yelling?" Joaquin, Gael, and Hugo stood at the door, and all I wanted to do was escape before everything blew up.

"She's talking about divorcing you. I'm more loyal to you than your wife, and you want to ship me off!" Alessandra pouted and crossed her arms over her chest.

Joaquin narrowed his eyes at Sofia and gazed over at his kids. My mouth went dry in nervousness. The anticipation of World War III in front of my face was something I hadn't planned on doing.

Boom!

"Arghhh!!!"

Everything happened in slow motion, and I prayed the kids' lives would be spared. Joaquin leapt over like Superman and covered the children, Gael reached out for Alessandra and tugged her down. I watched Sofia crawl to the kids, and Hugo went into attack mode and shot back. I couldn't believe what I was in the middle of. I knew right there that my life would be forever changed.

Pop! Pop!

"Arghhhh!!" I screamed, watching Joaquin grab both babies. Sofia stood as the bullets stopped.

"We need to go to the basement," Joaquin commanded.

"Where's Martha and the rest of the staff?" Sofia called out, and we ran out of the living room and through the hallway to the basement door. We saw Martha holding the door open.

"Mr. Fuertes! We saw at least five or six men," Martha explained.

"Gael, where are you going?" Alessandra pleaded, holding on to his jacket. He kissed the side of her face as the tears pooled into her eyes.

"Go with Martha. I'm right behind you," Gael told her.

"No!" Alessandra screamed.

"Alessandra! Ti amore." Gael gripped her palm and kissed her on the lips.

We ran through the basement and down to another door underground. I felt like I was in a movie. Sofia never told me about the basement or any of these compartments underneath the house.

"Let's go!" Joaquin shouted and held tight on to both crying babies as they screamed for their mom.

"Joaquin, how much further?" Sofia reached for Jianna, and Joaquin nudged her along, not breaking his stride.

"Right here." He typed in the keypad on the wall, and the door opened to the outside. We stepped out to a helicopter, and I looked back over my shoulder and saw we were miles away from the house.

"What about Hugo?" I asked.

"He knows the rules."

Joaquin buckled the kids into the plane. Another guy got in the front seat. Sofia climbed in the helicopter, and I looked back for Hugo and hesitated.

"Cassidy, come on," Sofia muttered.

"I can't leave him."

"He's fine. They're securing the house and will meet us at our location," Joaquin explained.

"How do you know?" I questioned.

"I know my men," Joaquin said.

"Cassidy, he's fine."

"We have to go!" During her sobs, Alessandra covered her face with her hands.

"Joaquin." As Sofia reached for his hands, he raised them to his mouth and kissed her palm.

"Martha, I thought you were a cook," I inquired.

"I am a cook and house manager," Martha replied.

"She's trained on how to handle things in case I'm not home," Joaquin explained, and I saw her in a different way. The woman had to be damn near in her late sixties.

"What about the rest of your staff?" I watched as the helicopter flew in the opposite direction of the house. I prayed Hugo and Gael came out of this alive.

"I have safety measures in place," Joaquin responded, and I stared at the houses as they got smaller the higher we flew up.

SOFIA

A few hours later, we occupied the second home Joaquin owned under his parents' name, and I showered, fed the kids, and stood in his office, watching him pace back and forth and yell on his phone. I couldn't understand all of what he was saying since he was possibly cursing, but he seemed angrier than usual. The last scare of my kidnapping set him on a rampage, and now for his kids to almost be killed, my husband wasn't the same man standing in front of me anymore. He'd changed, and I needed to understand that getting him back to the guy I fell in love with would be a struggle. The front door chirped, and I looked over and saw Gael and Hugo stalking in with dirty, angry faces. I reached to hug them both, and Cassidy practically leaped into Hugo's arms.

"You're alive!" Cassidy shouted.

"Cassi, everything is okay." Hugo held her close, and something tugged at my heart to see Hugo so vulnerable and open in front of me. Usually, it was me being a big baby, but he let his guard down with Cassidy.

"You okay?" Gael questioned.

"I'm fine."

"Where's Alessandra?"

"In the kitchen with the kids."

"Don't worry, he's going to be fine," Gael said.

"I hope so."

"Let me check on the kids and Alessandra," Gael said, and I nodded.

"Sofia, you can't get rid of me that easy." Hugo chuckled, and I slapped him on the chest.

"I'm glad you're safe."

"Me too." He kissed me on the forehead.

"How did you get out?" I questioned.

"Prayer, but it was just a warning message."

"A bomb was a warning message?" Cassidy probed.

"I need to discuss some things with Joaquin." Hugo gripped his chin and kissed her on the lips.

"How do you live like this?" Cassidy questioned.

"I love him."

"What are we going to do about Texas?"

"Joaquin won't let me leave the grounds, let alone finish filming."

"This is not good."

"Maybe they can figure out how to get the people behind this sooner."

"I think I'm going to be sick." Cassidy held her hands to her stomach and mouth.

She ran off to the bathroom, and I chased behind her and held her hair as she threw up in the toilet.

"Have you eaten?" I asked.

`She shook her head, flushed the toilet, and went to the sink to brush her teeth and rinse her mouth out.

"Have you and Hugo been careful?" I asked.

Her eyes bugged out. She groaned and covered her face in shame.

"My life can't be this crazy right now."

"It might seem like it's crazy, but you're only making it worse. Calm down, I have a test you can take."

"How do you go day to day in this lifestyle and not freak out?"

"You make it work." I opened the cabinet, grabbed a pregnancy test, and handed it to her.

"You have these just randomly around here?"

"Joaquin told me about the home a few months back after having Jianna, and I made sure to get everything we would need in case of emergencies."

"A pregnancy test is an emergency?"

"He wanted more kids, and I didn't know what I wanted, so we compromised."

"What do you mean compromised?"

"After Jianna, I said let me have a career for a little while. If we still wanted another child in two years, we could try."

"And."

I waved the tears away before they fell.

"After today, I can't do this again."

`Cassidy dropped the test on the counter and held me in her arms for a tight hug.

"Talk to him."

"I will, but first you need to take a test."

"Hugo and I as parents is nuts."

I laughed and shrugged.

"I said the same thing about Joaquin, but he's the most supportive when I'm pregnant and with the kids."

"Let me get this over with."

Bang! Bang!

"Sofia!" Alessandra yelled.

"My other child is knocking." I groaned and opened the door to Alessandra in tears.

"Don't make me go back." Alessandra dropped to her knees.

"What's happened now?"

"She's friends with my enemy." Joaquin's tone dropped low and deadly.

"Huh?"

"I didn't know!" Alessandra cried out. Gael reached down to pick her up.

"Get her out of here!" Joaquin shouted.

"Joaquin, tell me what's going on. She's your sister."

"She betrayed me." He glared at her.

"Joaquin, you know Alessandra would never do anything to betray the family." Gael calmly held her in his arms and brushed a hand up and down her back.

"Get her out of my face," Joaquin spat.

"Someone tell me what is going on."

"Alessandra's report from the drugs found in her system were traced back to a woman named Odessa," Gael explained.

"So?"

"Odessa Lusting is the sister of Emile Lusting, the man who blew up our home!" Joaquin shouted.

"I didn't know!" Alessandra begged.

I covered my mouth in shock.

"Alessandra."

She reached for my hand, and I took a step back.

"Get her out of my sight!" Joaquin yelled.

"We met in class, and she approached me. We became friends with Sofia." Gael held Alessandra.

"We've been set up all along. Alessandra brought her friend to our house." The right vein on the side of Joaquin's neck popped.

"I remember her being at the house," I recalled, closing my eyes.

. . .

FLASHBACK.

A month prior.

I was out by the pool, lounging with the kids and running through my lines with Madelyn. Cassidy was there to finalize details of my upcoming schedule.

"Sofia! Sofia! You look amazing." Alessandra held a mimosa in her hand and stood in front of the canopy lounge chair.

"What are you two doing today?" I dropped the script on the ground and stood to hug her.

"Sofia, this is my friend Odessa. We met in class." Alessandra introduced me, and I shook her hand. She was a tall woman, with a sharp jawline, heart-shaped lips, and long blond hair.

"Nice to meet you, Sofia. I'm a big fan," Odessa said.

"Thank you."

"I told her about your pool, and she suggested we come hang out. Plus, you have the best food," Alessandra joked.

"Help yourselves, please. Odessa, this is Cassidy."

"Hi," Cassidy said.

She ignored Cassidy.

"Those are your two kids?" Odessa asked.

"Yes."

"Beautiful, they look just like their father," Odessa hinted, and I didn't know if I should be offended or thankful.

"Uhm... thanks."

"Odessa's just joking," Alessandra said.

"How did you meet again?" I probed.

"In class, I cheated off her design!" Odessa cackled and clinked glasses with Alessandra.

I pursed my lips and glanced at Cassidy.

"She's joking. We met in class and became friends."

"Are you the one who keeps her out at all hours of the night?"

She pressed her index finger to her lips.

"Shush… you're not going to snitch on us, are you?"

"Mommy! Look at me!" JJ called out, and I looked away from Odessa.

"Can I use your restroom?" Odessa perked up, and I nodded.

"Sure, I can show you." I stood.

"Oh, no need. Just point me in the direction," Odessa said.

"Right through the doors you came from and around the corner," I responded and motioned to the house.

"Thanks! Be right back," Odessa replied, placing her mimosa on the ground.

"How long have you known her, Alessandra?"

She shrugged her shoulders.

"A few weeks, why?" Alessandra sipped on her drink.

"I don't know. Just feel a weird vibe from her."

"Odessa's really funny and sweet. Give her a chance," Alessandra responded.

"Food is ready!" Martha called out.

"Where's my brother?" Alessandra strolled next to me to the kitchen.

I grabbed a plate of hot dogs and burgers for JJ and a bottle for Jianna as Alessandra fixed a plate for herself. Cassidy came behind and took JJ's plate out of my hand.

"Thanks, I'll make you a plate," I told her.

"No worries, I'm stuffed from the snacks," Cassidy mentioned.

"Alessandra, I'm sorry I can't stay." Odessa stepped into the kitchen with a harsh grimace on her face.

"Why? What's wrong?"

"My guy needs me, and I have to run home to help him get in my apartment."

"How old are you, Odessa?"

"Why?" Her eyes darkened with her sharp response.

"Just asking. I know Alessandra is twenty-two, and her parents would go crazy if she lived with a man." I chuckled.

"Well, I'm not Alessandra." She slid her shades on, and I hugged Alessandra, turning to leave the kitchen.

"Maybe you should do a background check on her?" Cassidy mentioned.

"You two are being silly," Alessandra blurted out.

"Is she the reason you've been out all night and missing classes?"

"Sofia, can we have a peaceful day without all the questions?"

"Does Joaquin know your little friend?" I investigated.

"No, and I don't want him to know."

"She seems rude," Cassidy said.

"Odessa is nice, and I'm done talking about my personal life," Alessandra said as she dropped the spoon into the salad and marched out of the kitchen to the backyard.

ALESSANDRA

$\mathcal{P}$resent Day.

The look in my brother's eyes was like a sharp dagger to his heart. I didn't know how we could come back from this betrayal. The rising and falling of his chest, the darkening of his eyes, and the pain in his tone meant I'd done more than disappoint him this time. I was the cause of an enemy getting close and almost killing his family.

"Get the fuck out of my house!" Joaquin shouted, stalking out of the living room. I tried to run after him, but Gael held me back.

"No! You don't understand. He has to listen to me."

"Gael, take her away," Sofia said, and my heart broke at her words, I looked around the room at Hugo's Cassidy's sad eyes.

"Hugo, you have to believe me. I didn't know."

He shook his head.

"We should go." Gael gripped my elbow and angled me toward the door.

"Wait! Can I say goodbye to JJ and Jianna? Please, Sofia?" I begged.

She waved me off.

"I love them and would never hurt them."

"You should have thought of that before!" Sofia screamed, and I nodded, understanding my decisions affected the family in a way I couldn't undo.

"Come on," Gael repeated, and I let him walk me out of the house. I stopped and glanced at the family as tears pooled in my eyes.

"I am sorry."

* * *

I PACKED up my things and loaded them in the car, while Gael continued to talk to Joaquin on my behalf. This was not only hard on me but him as well. I swallowed the lump in my throat and closed my eyes. As I sat in the back of the car, I thought of how Odessa had made it her mission to be my friend. All of my life was planned for me, and I thought if I could come to America and make my own decisions and make friends, I would feel normal. My family could see I could handle my life without being constantly watched by guards and hounding me about the people coming in and out of my place. Odessa was friendly and flirty, but fun and outgoing. She never gave off a sign that she was a part of the mafia world. The door opened, and Gael scooted in and covered my hand, lifting it to his lips.

"Give him time."

"When can I come back?"

"Let's not think about that right now."

"Do you hate me?"

Gael turned toward me and raised his right hand to my

cheek. He caressed it and leaned over to press a kiss on my lips.

"Love you, baby, but disappointed."

"How much damage is done?"

He sighed and ran a hand through his dark, short, wavy hair.

"A lot we have to clean up."

"Are you coming with me?"

"To help you get settled in, but I can't stay long." He released my hand and grabbed his phone to scroll through messages.

"Did he tell my parents?"

"No way to keep this from them."

"That bitch needs to die."

I glanced out the window as the car drove down the street.

"You said you met her in class?"

"Yeah, she came in one day while we were designing and sat next to me."

"How did she come across?"

"Nice, Gael. I'm not Joaquin; I don't go around thinking everyone is out to get me."

"Alessandra!" He slammed his hand against the window. I jumped in shock, and tears welled up again.

"You hate me too."

"No, I want you to go back home and rethink your decision. You're trying to run away from this life, and there's no running, bella." He slid his hand on my thigh and squeezed. When we arrived at the airstrip, the door opened, and I hopped out in a somber mood, followed him toward the stairs, and climbed in to take a seat near the window. I buckled my seatbelt, and Gael sat across from me and watched me.

"Give him time," Gael said.

I nodded and blew out a breath.

"Hello, Miss Fuertes. Do you need anything to drink?" the flight attendant asked.

"A glass of wine please."

"Bring her water."

"Gael."

"You've had enough."

"Sure, water it is. And you, sir?" she questioned.

"Water please," Gael answered.

The stewardess walked off and left us alone.

"I didn't know I had drugs in my system," I whispered.

"Obviously she was drugging you," Gael told me, and I bit on my bottom lip, thinking of the night with Rich and Odessa.

"Now that I'm thinking about it, she always ordered the drinks for us."

"Alessandra, you're smarter than you give yourself credit for, and the woman I know wouldn't fall for the bullshit."

I started to speak and closed my mouth and stared out of the window.

"My father is going to kill me."

"Take it one day at a time."

"Here's your water. We'll be taking off shortly." Gael removed the seatbelt, switched to the seat next to me, and placed his arm around my shoulder. I leaned my head down on his chest and closed my eyes, taking in his clean, crisp cologne.

"She was plotting on me this whole time."

"Did she ever introduce you to Emile?"

"No, I only met a few guys around her. One guy was Rich."

He grunted in disapproval, and I pushed off his chest.

"I never cheated on you, Gael. He did kiss me, but I pushed him away."

"I trust you, baby."

The pilot came on and let us know he was about to take off. I leaned back on his chest and closed my eyes to sleep the last few hours away. We had a long flight, and I needed to be prepared for when I saw my parents again.

"Hi, I'm Odessa, your designs are gorgeous." She pointed at my open sketchbook.

"Thanks. I'm Alessandra."

"How long have you been designing?"

"All my life honestly."

"Everyone in here seems stuck up, except you." Odessa looked around the room.

I chuckled and pressed my index finger to my lips to be quiet.

"What? It's true. You're the only one who has talked to me since being here."

"I felt the same way when I first started here and getting my family to agree with me living here and designing clothes."

"Same, my family is very old fashioned."

"Seriously, they want you to marry rich and not have a career," I complained.

"Class, make sure you have the red cocktail dress sketch for next week." Our professor dismissed us for the day. I started to pack up my things to eat and meet Gael for dinner.

"Where are you off to now?"

I checked my watch.

"Grab something to eat and then meet my boyfriend."

"We should have lunch together."

"Uhmmm."

"Come on, you're too pretty to eat alone. Besides, I need to know who does your hair."

"Your hair is longer than mine and prettier."

"These blondie locks aren't real," she whispered in my ear and giggled.

"Lips are zipped. Come on, let's go for lunch."

Odessa locked her arm in mine, and we talked about every-thing as we went out for lunch that day and became fast friends.

* * *

A FEW DAYS later in Spain.

I could hear through the walls the loud shouts from my father and mother, going back and forth about me. We lived in a massive compound on acres of land, and I couldn't avoid the conversations that would happen once he saw me. When we arrived, I unpacked my clothes and went straight to bed. Gael was at his family home and would see me soon, but he had a few meetings he needed to handle before he could spend any time together. Without even knocking, my father forced his way into my room.

"Get downstairs now!" Father shouted in Portuguese.

"Papa."

"Joaquin Sr., leave her alone," Mother called out.

"Alba, stay out of this," he demanded.

"I'm coming."

I slipped on my flat sandals, grabbed my shawl, and followed behind him out of my room and toward his office.

"Are you hungry, sweetie?" Mother asked.

"No, I'm fine, Mommy."

"Do you know how this family runs?"

My head stayed down as he berated me.

"Yes, Papa."

"This makes us look weak! Stupid little girl," Father shouted.

"Stop it! You will not talk to our daughter like that. She made a mistake." Mother stepped in front of his face.

"Momma, it's okay."

"No, I will handle Alessandra. You made these problems before she was even born," Mother remarked.

"Alba, you will not interfere with me disciplining my children."

"She is not a little kid, Joaquin."

"Alessandra will be getting married."

My body trembled in shock as I gasped.

"No, I will not!"

"You've been making a lot of stupid mistakes; you can't handle the world on your own."

"Alessandra, go to your room," Mother said.

"I love Gael, and he loves me!" I yelled and stomped out of his office. I ran up to my bedroom, locked the door, and fell on my bed, crying over how my life had spiraled out of control and my father was going to force me to follow his rules.

JOAQUIN

$\mathcal{M}$y sister was back in my father's home country. I'd kept in touch with my father and explained how we were attacked. The conversation didn't go well, and he wondered if I needed to come back and start my business over. But I never ran from a fight. I sat on the back patio of our second home in thought, smoking on a cigarette to clear my head. Emile had made the first move on my territory, and then he blew up my home to bring me to my knees to sell a piece of what we had. Fuertes never got intimidated. When I killed my enemies, I went for the last bloodline. Our tech guy sent Odessa's address, and I made plans to visit her today.

"How long have you been out here?" Sofia asked.

I felt her warm hands massage my shoulders.

"An hour."

"Are you coming to bed?"

"Not anytime soon."

We'd finished dinner and put the kids to bed. It was still early, only nine p.m. I didn't have Gael, but Hugo would follow me on my mission.

"Come to bed, Joaquin." She ran a hand down the back of my neck. I closed my eyes, reached up for her hand, and pulled her in front of me.

"I'll be up to bed soon."

"I need to talk to you about something."

She sat in my lap, and I rubbed her back.

"I have to fly out to Texas."

"Not now, sweetheart."

"It's important."

"I said no."

"I understand your business is complicated, but you can send more men with me and the kids."

"My kids aren't going anywhere."

"Are you fighting me on this? I've always done my work."

"I'm not stopping you."

"What do you call making us stay in an undisclosed location and away from my family and friends?"

"Your parents can visit, and Cassidy is here all the time."

"You sent your sister away, and now you're trying to lock me up."

"Sofia, you know you're important to me."

"Sometimes it doesn't feel that way when you're demanding me to follow your rules."

I rubbed her cheek and down to her chin.

"Only want you safe."

"How were we able to get so close to our house?"

"Odessa had to have given the address."

"Are you going to kill her?"

"Go to bed." I gripped her chin, captured her lips, and slid my tongue through her full lips.

"Hmmmm… stay out here," she moaned, and I picked her up. She wrapped her legs around my waist, and I walked her in the house through the kitchen and down the hall to the guest bedroom. I locked the door and placed her on her back. I kissed the back of her ankle, and my dick jumped when she rubbed her left foot up my stomach and down to my balls.

"I can't deny you anything," I whispered. Hovering over her body, I buried my face in the crook of her neck. She wrapped her legs around my waist, slipped her hand in my pants, and gripped my shaft.

"Ohhh… Make love to me," she croaked out.

She kissed down my shoulder and up to my jaw as I squeezed her right breast in my hand.

"You ready for me, mi amore?"

"Yes… please."

Her nectar dripped onto the sheets, and I slipped her panties to the side under her robe, lined up my thick girth to her tight walls, and plunged deep. I couldn't speak for a second as she gripped me on both sides of my ass and arched her back.

"Ughh… Sofia."

"Oh… God!" she begged. I paced slowly, widened her legs, and watched her arousal overshadow her beautiful face. Her breath hitched, and that was my cue to take her over the edge. I slid my finger to her clit, grabbed both legs, and closed them together, straight up in the air. Raising my hips, I pounded her against the bedpost as our combined moans filled the room. I became aggressive, feeling that I had lost her. My chest rose and fell, and my vision became blurred as I thought about what we had just gone through and how I could have lost her. Taking her into my arms, I sucked on her neck as my hands roamed over every inch of her body.

"Sweetheart, I need you."

"You have me, Joaquin."

"Never leave me." My hand went to her throat, and I stared into her eyes.

"You have me forever."

"Do you promise?"

"I promise... baby!"

"Baby, I'm coming."

"Come for me, my love."

"Shit!"

* * *

THIRTY MINUTES LATER, I cocked the gun, checked our surrounding area, and pulled the ski mask over my head.

"Is she alone?" I asked Steven.

"She was."

"If she isn't, it's lost there." I opened the door, put the gun in my back, and headed into the apartment building. Surprisingly, it was near my sister's condo. They'd thought about everything when they planned to take over, except my retaliation wouldn't be a normal one and done. I planned to have his business destroyed within a few minutes of me taking his sister from this earth. Hugo followed me to the back entrance of the building, and we slipped through the doors that were left open by the security guard we had paid off. I opened the side stair doors and quietly went up to her third floor. Peeking out the window, I confirmed it was clear, and I grabbed the gun from behind my back and removed the safety.

"If she's not alone, take out whoever is with her."

"Ready to go," Hugo said, cocking his gun. Thinking about the noise my gun would make, I passed it to Hugo and removed my knife from my ankle. I pressed my head to the door and didn't hear anything, so I slid my hand in my pants pocket and took out the key to her apartment and pushed in to quietly open her door. I saw the living room was dark, so I waved Hugo to follow and look at the other side of the apartment. Her kitchen was open floor with a balcony attached. I went down the hall and saw three doors. I figured one was a bathroom. Hugo eased the door open and saw it was empty.

He mouthed, *Clear.*

I pointed for him to check the other room in the corner, and I'd take the main room on the count of three. Holding my hand up, on three, I pushed it open and saw Odessa lying in bed alone with the window open. I grinned, pulling on my black leather gloves, stalked to her bed, and pressed my hand over her mouth. Her eyes popped open.

"Arghhhh!" she screamed.

"Sshhh… Odessa, correct?"

Her eyes widened in surprise. I removed my ski mask so she could see my face.

"You've been a very bad girl, Odessa."

She shook her head and tried to claw my hands down.

"You listen, and I speak."

Odessa nodded.

"Your brother Emile, where is he?"

"Mmhmm…"

"I'm going to remove my hand so you can talk, but the second you scream, I'll kill you." I held the knife up to her jaw. "Understand?"

"Mmmmm."

"Where is your brother?"

"He gets in contact with me."

"I don't believe you."

"Please, he made me do that."

"I think you're right that he planned to take my family down."

"I swear I'm innocent," she pleaded as tears welled up in her eyes.

I chuckled, and Hugo came in the room next to me. Odessa tried to crawl out of the bed, and I caught the back of her head and yanked her back.

"Please! I don't know anything."

"Normally, I leave the killing to my friends, but you've made the biggest mistake, so I have to handle this alone."

"If you let me go, I can get my brother for you."

I laughed.

"Alessandra was foolish, but I am not. You can't manipulate me."

"If you kill me, this will be a war!" she shouted and tried to kick me in the balls. I smacked her across the face, lifted the knife, and held it up to her face.

"One move, and you die."

Odessa grinned.

"My brother will avenge me. The Lusting family doesn't fall to your kind," she spat.

"Too bad you won't be here to see it fail." I slid the knife across her throat. She tried to catch the blood but choked on it and died.

"Any signs of her brother's address?"

"Nothing."

"We need to go to the club."

We texted Gabriella to clean up the scene while we left to handle the next location Emile was seen. Steven was at the wheel of the car and jumped in the passenger side and waved for me to drive.

"She gave up the address?" Steven questioned.

"No, try the club now."

"They hit some of his men," Steven said.

"He'll show his face soon." I removed the ski mask, wiped off the knife, and grabbed the gun back from Hugo.

"If he's not there?"

"Keep looking. Sofia has to go to Texas, and I'm not taking any chances."

"Are you going with her?"

"That would be ideal, but until this is handled, I can't."

"The kids?"

"I want them protected at all times, but they're staying here with me."

He sped down the street, and we made it to the club of the shootout and parked two blocks away.

SOFIA

Two days later.

I'd been out in Texas for two days, working with Shamar and doing press, while Joaquin was back home, doing what he did. The director was doing a shoot on location with a few of us, and I'd been trying to get in touch with Joaquin for the longest time. Madelyn kept me updated about the kids, but Joaquin hadn't come up late at night and left early in the morning. Some women would think he was cheating, but I knew my husband. Dating another woman would never enter his mind.

"All right, we're almost losing the light. Get this shot!" the director called out.

The makeup artist touched up my lipstick and held the small fan up to get air while we were outside the trailers, preparing to film. I read over my lines one more time, passed them back to the assistant, and stepped on the gravel near Shamar.

"So this scene is you stopping him from leaving," the director said.

"Should I be on the side of him, or do you want more of his face?"

"We can try both angles."

Shamar leaned back on the car door, and I placed my hands on my hips, moving my head left to right. I closed my eyes to drown out the noise of the world.

"Action!"

"Listen to me, if you leave now, our relationship won't mean a thing."

"Stop lying to yourself!" he shouted.

"So that's it… just forget about the nights we've spent together." I pushed my hand on his chest.

"Sorry, I need to go." He turned and went to open the driver's side.

"Cut!" the director shouted.

"Should we do one more take?"

"We can break for five and then come back."

Shamar grabbed the robe from the assistants, and we walked to our trailers. Cassidy passed me a bottle of water and the fan as I turned the knob of the trailer, stepping up the stairs to sit under the air.

"Have you heard from Hugo?"

"Yeah, anything from Joaquin?" Cassidy questioned.

I shook my head.

"No."

"He's probably doing what he does."

"That's what I fear."

"Give him time, Sofia."

"I miss my babies."

"We won't be much longer, and you'll fly back soon."

"Can you get the interviews in one day?"

"Let me see, and I'll talk to them about doing something closer to the premiere."

"I just have a bad feeling with everything going on."

"Any word from Alessandra?"

"Her mother called and told us she made it all right, and Gael should be on his way back."

"I'm still surprised so much has gone down, and we're alive to speak."

"No fear in marrying Hugo."

"A lot of fear, but I love him too much."

"I understand, and the only advice I can give is to be intentional with every moment."

"We have too much going good to be down right now."

"How are the numbers looking?"

Cassidy turned the computer around.

"Well, after the uproar with the studio trying to cut you from the movie, your social presence has increased."

"Really?"

"Yes, women especially are rooting for you."

"The magazine."

"The sales are through the roof, and they're even thinking of a second shoot."

"No more photos of my kids though."

"Understandable, but they want to know more about Joaquin."

"Because of the photos and sex tape?"

"Yes."

"I knew it. All these gossip bloggers think about is getting into people's private lives."

"Just let me know what you want to do."

"I'll finish up this shoot and do the interviews tomorrow."

"Do we want to have dinner tonight?"

"The hotel would be fine."

"Okay."

A knock on my trailer door came.

"Back on set!" someone yelled out.

"Be right there."

I checked myself out in the mirror and went to open the door, strolling back to set to finish the scene of the day.

* * *

THE NIGHT BREEZE in the restaurant of the hotel was exquisite, and I felt my cheeks blush in thinking of me and Joaquin here on our honeymoon. We hadn't been accosted by any fans, for the most part, but a few cameras did go off. I asked the wait staff to ask people to keep them at a minimum. Cassidy couldn't make the dinner, so Shamar was here, and we'd so far caught up on everything in our lives.

"What do you have planned after this movie?" I cut into my vegetables and rice.

"A film I'm looking forward to producing, maybe some TV."

"Can you believe the mess Pamela tried to pull?"

I lifted my glass of wine.

"She's relentless."

"She acts like I want my private life in the public."

His hand brushed over my palm.

"People like Pamela are only out for themselves."

"That's what I hate about this celebrity life."

"Mrs. Fuertes," the smooth voice interrupted, and I glanced up to a tall man with a bald head and a thin mustache and wearing a black suit.

"Yes."

"I'm a friend of your husband." He reached out for a shake.

I gulped down the wine.

"Joaquin."

"Yes, he'd informed me that you were here in town and asked that I make myself known."

"What's your name?" My emotions were high on alert, and I was ready to bolt out of the restaurant if he was an enemy of Joaquin's.

"Ezequiel Mota." He winked, and I gazed over at Shamar.

"Uhm, Mr. Mota, it's nice to meet you. This is my friend Shamar."

"You have to forgive me, I'm not really big on movie actors." Ezequiel removed his hat and held it to his chest.

"No, problem at all," Shamar replied.

"What can I help you with, Mr. Mota?"

"It's more of what I can do for you."

"I'm sorry?"

"Have you spoken to your husband?"

I didn't know if this was a setup, or he really worked with my husband; the last time I trusted one of his people, I'd ended in trouble.

"I have," I lied.

"Then you know I'm here on good faith. Protection," he hinted and placed his hat back on his head.

"Shamar and I are having dinner. Besides, I have protection." I pointed to the guards sitting at the table behind us that Joaquin had demanded I have.

"I understand, but my protection is at the level of your husband's. I have connections here so if you come up with any issues—"

"I doubt anything will happen while I'm in Texas." I chuckled.

"You can never be too careful." He slid a right hand in his pocket, pulled out a business card, and left on the table.

"I'll remember that, Mr. Mota."

I stared at the name and number on the card and put it in my clutch.

"That was strange." Shamar lifted his wine glass to his lips.

I nodded and glanced at the door of the restaurant again.

"Anything else you two need?" The waitress stepped over, removed the check, and put it on the table.

"No, we're great. Thank you." I started to remove my wallet, but Shamar put his card down.

"It's my treat," Shamar said.

"Thanks, Shamar." I stood, and the guards approached me, ready to leave.

"Tomorrow, we have interviews," Shamar said.

"Cassidy should be lining up flights for me to fly back home."

"Did they say anything about the explosion at your place?"

We walked out of the restaurant and stopped at the valet. The guard passed my ticket to get the keys to our car.

"No, the press is crazy and throwing so many lies out there."

"Glad the studio didn't cut you out of the movie." He leaned over and gave me a hug when a flash went off.

"*Shamar and Sofia! Are you in love?*" a photographer yelled out.

I blocked my eyes from the bulb flashes, jogged to the car, and climbed in when more reporters gathered around it.

"Can we go!" I shouted and held my head down.

* * *

BANG! Bang!

I groaned and tightened the covers around my head to block out the loud noise.

Bang! Bang!

"Cassidy!" I shouted.

I heard loud noises and whispers.

"You can't go in there." Cassidy's raised voice.

The bedroom door was pushed open, and I jumped in surprise.

"Mrs. Fuertes?"

I pulled the blanket close to my body.

"Yes."

My heart raced at the police standing in my room with guns drawn.

"You're wanted for questioning."

"I'm sorry. What is this about?"

"Don't say anything, Sofia. Let me call Joaquin," Cassidy stated.

The slimy smirk on the cop in front of me with eyes narrowed in slits, tall with a wide gut, dark hair, and front gold tooth creeped me out. He stepped closer to my bed and tossed down a piece of paper.

"This can't be true." I flipped the paper back and forth in disbelief, seeing Shamar was dead.

"You're an actress, no?"

"Who are you?"

"I'm the captain of police."

"I'm not going anywhere until I speak to my lawyer."

"Your money won't buy you freedom."

Cassidy tried to approach the bed, but one of the cops blocked her from coming farther.

"I've done nothing wrong, so this is a lie." I dropped the paper on the floor.

"Get dressed. You need to answer some questions since you're the last one to see him alive."

"Do you know who I am?"

He smirked.

"Like I said, you have five minutes, or my men will drag you out." He turned and motioned for his men to follow him.

The door shut, and Cassidy reached for her phone. I jumped out of bed to get dressed.

"What the hell is going on?" I whispered, opened the door slightly, and looked in the living room at them talking amongst themselves, touching our things.

"Why would I kill someone?"

"The studio sent out a public statement and said everything is on hold." Cassidy scrolled through her phone.

I grabbed a shirt and pants from my luggage.

"Where is my phone?" I tossed clothes out of my bag and remembered my phone was left in my clutch out in the living room.

"Shit!" I hissed.

"What?" Cassidy bit her nail, holding the phone up to her ear.

"My phone is out there in my purse."

"I'm trying to get a hold of production."

"I need to get Joaquin on the phone."

Knock! Knock!

"Mrs. Fuertes, your time is up!"

"Give me a second."

"No one is answering the phone." Cassidy ended the call.

"You don't think something happened to them?"

"Whoever is behind this wants you and Joaquin to suffer," Cassidy remarked, and I slid a hand through my disheveled hair and nodded in agreement.

"The same person who set the explosion at our house."

"No more waiting. Time to go!" He barged into my room and startled us.

"All right, let me grab my shoes."

"I'm coming with her," Cassidy said.

"No."

"She's my manager, and I don't even know if you're a real cop," I spat, and he stalked over and closed the distance between us.

"Your husband may have pull in New York but not here." He gripped my arm tight and dragged me out of the bedroom.

"You're hurting my arm!" I shouted.

"All you spoiled American women make me sick." He pushed me toward the other guard, and I noticed my purse was in his hand.

"I have a right to call a lawyer," I demanded.

He shrugged.

"We'll think about it."

Cassidy followed behind us as he walked me out of the room and onto the elevator. I didn't even get a chance to clean myself up. I felt like a prisoner all over again like the last time. Somehow, this was much worse. The elevator opened, and crowds of people from reporters and guests took photos of me while he paraded me out like a criminal.

"Sofia Fuertes, do you have anything to say to Shamar's family?" A reporter stuck a mic in front of my face.

"Sofia, over here!" another photographer yelled.

SOFIA

The dingy room was dark, dusty, and smelled of rotten food and blood everywhere. Our time in Texas should have been a way for me to become more than a pretty face, and I was now in handcuffs at the police station about my costar. The door opened, and the same cop from earlier walked in with a smile on his face. He sat in the chair in front of me, crossed his legs, and lit a cigarette.

"You smoke?"

"No," I muttered.

"Terrible habit." He chortled.

"When can I go?"

He flipped the file open and pushed a photo across the table. I leaned over and saw a picture of Shamar dead in the backseat of a car.

"What happened to him?"

He laughed, took the photo back, and shoved the photo of me and Shamar hugging at the valet station in my face.

"Come on, do us both a favor and tell the truth."

"Captain Herrera."

"Speak."

I cleared my throat.

"I don't know what happened to Shamar. I went to my hotel room after dinner. Plenty of people saw me walk into the hotel."

"That might be true, but you could have slipped out."

My heart was racing, and I shifted in my seat. This was a game to him, but my life was on the line, and obviously, he was looking for something.

"How much?"

Captain Herrera's eyes went wide.

"Excuse me?"

"You're not talking to some weak woman, Captain."

He put the cigarette out and leaned on the table with his hands clasped together.

"Money won't help you."

The door suddenly opened, and we both turned to see Ezequiel with Cassidy.

"Herrera… I thought we talked about this before." Ezequiel stepped in the room and picked up the picture of Shamar.

"She's not free to go."

"I have friends in high places, Herrera. You don't want to challenge me."

"Did he hurt you?" Cassidy asked.

"No."

"Release her now." Herrera pointed at my cuffed hands.

"A worthless scum like you doesn't give orders," Herrera fussed.

"As soon as I saw you go in the hotel this morning, I figured you'd pull something like this."

My head spun toward Mota.

"Hold up, you've watched my hotel?"

Mota nodded.

"My men and I kept tabs on you as soon as you came into town. Then, after the dinner, we followed you back."

"Do you know what happened to Shamar?" I asked.

"Herrera, Lusting can't keep you safe," Mota threatened.

Herrera jumped out of the chair, and it fell back.

"Are you threatening me?" Herrera pointed a finger at Mota.

"Everyone knows Lusting is behind you setting up Mrs. Fuertes."

"Captain! She's made bail, sir." Another cop walked in the room.

Captain Herrera's face grew heated, turning red in anger.

"This isn't over." Captain Herrera stood in Mota's face.

"I didn't kill anyone, Mr. Herrera."

"No need to explain to him, Mrs. Fuertes."

I rose from the chair and rubbed my wrists to relieve the pain.

"We'll be in contact about follow-up questions, Mrs. Fuertes," Herrera mentioned as we headed out of the inter-rogation room. I pushed through the crowds and kept my head down as Cassidy and Mota escorted me to a black van. I didn't know if we could trust him, but at this moment, I needed someone on my side to get me out of Texas.

The door shut, and Mota spoke to his men to drive off. He turned to look at me in the backseat and passed me my clutch.

"How did you get this back?" I questioned.

"Associate of mine."

I blew out a breath, opened it up, and removed my dead cell phone.

"Cassidy, what have you heard? My phone is dead."

"The entire situation is crazy. Shamar's car was found in a ditch."

"How is that possible!"

"It was set up by Lusting."

"The same man who tried to kill us?"

Mota nodded.

"He has reach, and after his sister was killed, it raised the stakes."

"His sister." I made eye contact with Cassidy.

"Odessa was found with her throat slit in bed," Mota replied.

"This is payback."

"I'm afraid your friend was caught in the middle."

"Framing me for his murder."

"They wanted to kill you as well, but you left before him."

The van drove back to the hotel, and I prayed I could get on the first flight out of here because if Herrera had his way he'd make me disappear to Mexico.

"Can you get us a flight out of here?"

"I will do my best." Mota reached in his pocket and removed his cell.

"Thank you."

"Hugo isn't answering his phone." Cassidy bit her bottom lip, staring out the window.

"Did Joaquin have something to do with Odessa dying?"

"I can't answer that question, Mrs. Fuertes."

"But you think it's payback, so more than likely, Joaquin sent a message."

* * *

As soon as the van dropped us off a few hours ago, I went to shower and change my clothes. Cassidy was calling the airlines to get us a flight out immediately, but everyone was booked for another two days. I didn't want to stay here and wait for Herrera to come back. I packed up my last bag and set it near the bedroom door. My stomach growled, and I remembered I hadn't eaten all day today. The press had a field day with the news of my arrest and made it seem like we were having an affair. On top of that, the studio and production team ignored my calls and acted like I was some piranha, putting out a blanket statement that they wished to wait until all the evidence had come out before determining any judgment. Cassidy sat on the couch next to me as Mota was on the phone yelling at someone.

"Any luck with Hugo?"

"Nothing."

"Do you think something happened to them?"

"We can't think like that."

"Joaquin has never gone a day without talking to me."

"We'll be home soon."

"I need to talk to my kids."

"Is your phone charged?"

"I couldn't get a signal."

"You think they did something to your phone?" Cassidy lowered her eyes, her breathing heightened.

"Something is going on, and we can't trust anyone."

Our eyes locked on Mota.

"Mrs. Fuertes, I have a private jet ready for you."

I jumped up in shock.

"Really... I can leave now?"

"Yes, I have word that some of Lusting's men are at the airport, so it's easier if we send you privately."

"Why are you doing this, Mota?"

"Your husband is a friend of mine."

"Have you spoken with him?"

"Not directly."

"So it's true… a war has started."

"Let me get you to the airport. Come, we have very little time." He looked at his watch.

"What about Shamar's body?"

"I'm afraid I can't help with that situation."

"But if we leave his body here, all of his family will think I'm guilty." My heart pounded in my chest

"Sofia, we need to leave, and I think Mota is right," Cassidy remarked.

"This is bad." My hands felt clammy.

"Let's just get out of here." Cassidy stood, grabbing her things.

As though my life were getting better, it all started to crash down again because of who I'd chosen to marry. I closed my eyes and said a little prayer for Shamar, then went to pick up my coat and bags to follow Cassidy out of the room. Ezequiel had a car waiting for us downstairs, and we locked the door, hopped on the elevator before it closed, and saw a couple of guys and one girl standing with drinks in their hands.

"Oh my God! Aren't you that actress who's accused of murder?" the redhead blurted out.

I swallowed the lump in my throat and covered my face with my hair.

"Shut up, Claire." The guy poked her in the arm. I was grateful he had a little more tact than his girlfriend. The elevator stopped in the lobby, and it was pretty quiet besides a few people checking in at this time of night. I followed behind Ezequiel, and his men were in the same black van as earlier. He took my bags as I jumped in and fastened my seatbelt.

"What about us checking out?"

"No worries. That was taken care of already."

"Thank God."

Ezequiel shut the door and jumped in the passenger side of the van. He waved for his man to drive off. My stomach growled, and I rubbed my belly, thinking of how my entire life had turned into a circus once again.

"How long do we have to get to the airport?"

"We're going through a shortcut," Ezequiel replied.

"Boss, we have company," the driver mentioned to Ezequiel. I turned to look out the window and saw a black SUV driving close behind us.

"Lose them," Ezequiel said, opening the glove compartment and taking out his gun.

"This can't happen."

"Stay calm. They would be stupid to do anything right now." Cassidy reached for my hand and squeezed it tight.

"We're going to be okay," Cassidy reassured me, and I nodded.

"Joaquin," I mumbled to myself.

Pop! Pop!

"Arghhh!" The car swerved, and my stomach dropped as I clambered to get low on the floor.

"Stay down!"

The driver cut into another lane, honked, and yelled about getting cut off. Ezequiel sent shots back, and the van sped up down the street.

"Take the back roads!" Ezequiel shouted.

Everything was quiet for another five minutes, and I sat up and looked out of the window, but I didn't see the car anymore. My hands shook, and my nerves were on edge as we continued to drive up on an abandoned dirt road.

"Where are we?" I asked, looking at the no trespassing sign and a dingy house with a broken-down car out front.

"Your private plane," Ezequiel replied, and the car

stopped. My eyes rose in surprise at the helicopter sitting behind the house.

"You have to be kidding me."

"Mrs. Fuertes, the only way you're getting home is with that plane."

"Come on, Sofia. It doesn't draw any attention." Cassidy unfastened her seatbelt.

"Who is flying the plane?"

"Me," Ezequiel stated.

"What!"

He chuckled.

"Your husband and I go way back. We've done business off and on."

"That doesn't mean I trust you to fly."

"I'm certified to fly, don't worry." Ezequiel held the door open and helped me out.

"What about the men shooting at us?"

"They'll be taken care of once you're gone."

"Joaquin knows about this plan?"

"Joaquin created the plan."

My stomach tightened at those words. So he knew what had taken place all this time, but he had ignored my calls and kept me in the dark. Ezequiel grabbed my bags, and I followed behind him to the helicopter. I placed the things in the corner, slid in the seat near the door, and sent a prayer up that I'd make it home in peace. The driver of the car got in on the other side, buckled his seatbelt, and started pushing buttons.

"Relax, Sofia; we're safe."

"How can you be so relaxed?"

"I know we wouldn't make it this far without Hugo and Joaquin protecting us."

I shook my head and wiped the tears that pooled in my eyes.

"Glad you have that much trust."

Ezequiel started the plane and threw a thumbs-up at us. I sat back with my hands clasped together in my lap and held on tight as I thought of ways to breathe without freaking out that something could happen. Five minutes later, the plane rose from the ground, and I shut my eyes tight. When I opened them, we were in the air. When I scanned the ground, I noticed two or three SUVs drive up and open the doors with guns in their hands.

JOAQUIN

Smack!

"I was arrested!" she shouted and raised her hand to smack me again, but I blocked her and tightened my grip. When we got to the house, I pulled Sofia into my office, and she yanked out of my hold and smacked me across the face. The hateful glare in her eyes broke my heart, and I wanted to kiss away the pain, but I couldn't be soft with her right now. She needed to understand where we were and what was next with Lusting.

Ezequiel had done as I asked and brought her home safely. It was going on eleven at night, and the kids were asleep in their beds. Cassidy stayed in the guestroom with Hugo, and Sofia was finally speaking to me, after ignoring me when we did the exchange at the small airport I owned. The look in her eyes was disappointment, and I promised I would never hurt her again, but the only way it would have worked was if I kept my contact to a minimum. I still hadn't gotten a hold of Lusting. When we went to the club, he wasn't there. We set it on fire, and that caused another ripple because he came back and reached Sofia in Texas. When I got word she was going no matter if I agreed or not, I had Ezequiel in place to watch over her. Keeping her from talking to the kids was another issue, but I couldn't let anyone tap into my lines or get wind of where we lived. I was foolish in thinking my family home couldn't be touched, but no longer would I rely on just my men. I called Carlo to send me some backup to watch over our home, and it was all on lockdown unless it was an emergency.

"Baby, I know, and I have my men taking care of the captain."

"What does that mean?"

The scowl on her face made me hesitant before I answered. I reached for her hand, and she jerked back.

"Captain Herrera works for Lusting."

"I know."

"It was a setup. I don't have all the evidence, but we think he killed Shamar as soon as you left."

"Odessa, did you kill her?"

"Yes."

She groaned and threw her hand up in the air.

"When will this stop, Joaquin? My God." She sat on the couch near the window.

I walked over and dropped to my knees in front of her.

"Sweetheart."

"Don't."

I tried to kiss her on the lips.

"I need to shower."

"Lusting is trying to come into my territory. I didn't agree, so he sent Odessa."

"I want you to leave this life alone."

"Listen to me."

"No." She jumped up to leave. I grabbed her arm, spun her around, and pulled her into my chest.

"You're my wife. I love you, but you will never dictate my business."

"I finally see what Sabrina was talking about."

"We're not them."

"No, you're worse." She shoved me away.

"Sofia." I ran up behind her and picked her up in a bear hug.

She kicked and yelled.

"Stop it!"

"Let me go."

"You'll wake the kids."

"He's dead, Joaquin."

"I know, sweetheart, and I apologize. We'll make Lusting pay."

"I'm going to be sick."

I walked her to the bathroom near my office, let her down, and held her hair back. She gagged, threw up, and sat on the floor for a few minutes.

"Tell me everything."

"Lusting has a cartel from France that wants to take over here."

"You said no."

"Not just me. Antonio, Carlo, and some friends have New York locked. We can't let anyone come in and take over."

"They used Alessandra, now me."

"It'll be over soon."

"Have you talked to your sister?" She stood to wash her face and brush her teeth.

"Not yet."

"What about your parents?"

"My father knows what's going on."

"I need to talk to my parents."

I shook my head. "Not right now."

She dropped the brush and turned to look at me.

"You think he'll go after my parents?"

"Safer to keep them out of this for right now."

"I don't like it when you ignore me, Joaquin."

She turned and finished brushing her teeth. I walked up and wrapped my arms around her waist, nuzzling my face in her neck.

"It wasn't on purpose."

Sofia spat out the toothpaste and rinsed her mouth out. I stood back as she wiped her hands and turned to face me.

"My career is over."

"We can fix that."

"How? More threats?" she hissed as she pushed me back, stormed out, and ran up the stairs to our bedroom.

"Sofia."

"Joaquin." I looked over at Cassidy.

"You should be asleep."

"Give her space," Cassidy said, crossing her hands over her chest.

"We never argued like this before."

"She's scared and upset, and I don't blame her."

"Herrera's going to get what's coming to him."

"He's a vile man. It was like he was having fun seeing her suffer."

My jaw clenched at her words.

"Did he touch her?"

"No… well, I don't know. He wouldn't let me see her."

"We couldn't make a move earlier, but I'll have some things in place for him."

"I think she should do an interview."

"No."

"Joaquin, what you're not getting is that her life has always been music and acting. Since she married you—"

"What are you saying?" My brows dipped in anger, forming a crease in my forehead.

"You might be a big-time mafia god, but when she married you, it didn't look like a good thing in the public's eyes."

"My life with Sofia isn't for the public."

"I get that, but they don't. Everything she does is picked apart and watched."

I waved off her comment.

"Listen, just let me set up an interview with you both, to clear the air and maybe savage her career."

"Not right now, Cassidy."

"Soon, it needs to happen soon if she has a chance of keeping her career stable." Cassidy turned and went back to the guest room. I sighed, ran a palm down my face, and went to our bedroom. Slipping my clothes off, I hopped in the shower and let the hot steam sprinkle down on my body to relax my muscles and take the stress away. I was making the wrong steps, and somehow Emile took me for a fool for giving in to his threats. Odessa didn't think she could be touched, and I needed to make a bigger statement than burning his club. I turned the water off, wrapped the towel around my waist, and walked out of the bathroom. Dropping the towel, I climbed in bed behind her and wrapped her in my arms. She tried to scoot out of my arms, and I tightened my grip.

"Joaquin, no," she mumbled.

"Sofia, please, sweetheart." I kissed her cheek and the side of her neck.

I rubbed a hand up and down her stomach.

"Just let me sleep."

"I love you, sweetheart. I would never put you in danger."

"You promise?"

She turned around in my arms.

"He will pay for what he tried to do to you."

"After that, you have to let it go."

I gritted my teeth.

"Go to sleep, baby." She caressed my cheek, and I lifted her hand to my mouth and kissed her wedding ring.

* * *

A FEW DAYS LATER, I agreed with Cassidy to let Sofia do an interview solo, as long as we had a chance to look at the questions first. I had Carlo's men follow her and Cassidy to the studio, while I was with Gabriella and Gael. Hugo was with us today and drove us to the warehouse. I held my cell and texted my father to check in on Alessandra.

Me: How is she?

Father: She's adjusting.

Me: How is Mother?

Father: She's pissed at me and you.

I smirked at his comment. Alba was a strong woman like Sofia and hated when certain decisions were made that would put the family in dangerous positions. Alessandra had betrayed our family, and I was too pissed to see she was a naïve girl who had been taken advantage of by Lusting's sister. After the hospital showed us the traces of drugs in her system, it sent me in a rage, and I felt Sofia was next on the list with the video being leaked. She'd suffered enough because of me, and I needed to realize that my choices weren't making things better.

Me: Tell her I'm sorry, and I love her.

Father: How are you moving with Lusting?

Me: I have dinner plans set up.

Father: Make sure the decision you make is the final one.

I sent him word in code that the final decision was dinner, and no one would leave the table alive now that I had the backing of Mota and the De Luca Cartel. They arrived at Antonio's. I stepped out, followed Gabriella and Gael once I ended my text message, and put my phone away.

Gael and I shook hands with Carlo and glared at Emile as he sat with a smile on his face.

"What's this?" I waved my hand around, feeling betrayed by my friends.

"It's not what you think," Carlo said.

I slid my hand behind me to reach for my gun. On cue, his men pulled their guns and pointed at my men.

"No blood today, boys." Carlo stepped in front of my gun.

"Carlo, I respect you and Antonio, but this is something I can't forgive."

"He seems unhappy to see me." Emile chuckled, and I growled, starting to charge at him. Gael pulled me back and whispered in my ear, "Not here."

"I called you both here to come up with an agreement," Carlo explained, picking up the shot glass and pushing it in my hand.

"I'm not drinking with him."

The smile dropped from his face.

"You killed my sister, and now you think I'm dirt on your shoes!" Emile smacked the table and jumped up.

"Fuck you and your sister!" I spoke in Italian.

"Gentleman, the only way we can settle this is by talking," Carlo demanded.

"I'm done talking. He made the first move, and I'll make the last."

"Joaquin."

I turned and saw Antonio standing at the entrance of the hallway.

"You knew about this?"

"We have certain things that could benefit Emile, and I think you should hear him out."

I cracked my knuckles and spoke in my native Portuguese.

"I see your friend doesn't want to make money." Emile lit a cigar.

"Emile, the way you approached him was wrong. We don't work like that in New York," Carlo explained. I was getting anxious and needed to see his blood spilled.

"How is your wife? She's a beautiful woman," Emile blurted out, his last words before I lifted my gun and shot two of his men in the head.

Pop! Pop!

He pushed the table up and sent gunshots back. Carlo and Antonio moved out of the way, shouting at us.

"Motherfucker! I'll kill you!" I yelled.

"She's a sexy woman, you should be proud," Emile continued to taunt, until he slipped out of the room as his men sent shots at us. Gabriella shot one of his guys in the leg, and Gael followed me toward the front entrance. We ran to the alley and saw him climb in a car. It backed up fast, coming at us as we sent bullets toward them. It was bulletproof and didn't make a dent. I jumped out of the way before they hit us. I dropped the gun and stood up as the car drove off and clenched my fist.

"We need to go before it gets hot," Gael said.

"I need to see Antonio and Carlo."

"Hurry, let's go."

We jogged back in and saw bullet holes in the walls.

Carlo held his arm, hurt from broken glass, while it was getting wrapped up.

"How deep is the wound?" I questioned.

"Just a graze," Carlo responded, taking the shot straight.

"You won't have to worry about Emile killing you," Antonio replied.

"What do you mean?"

"Soon as Janice hears he got shot because of you..." Antonio mentioned, and I grunted, not ready for that conversation. Sofia had taken on a lot of their traits, and I'd hate for her to be the gun-toting donna like Janice and Sabrina had become.

"I'll send her flowers."

"'You'll need to do more than that." Carlo chuckled.

"You both played it well."

They slapped hands with me, and I pulled out money to pay for the damages.

"This is for the repairs."

"No need to pay us, we knew this could happen," Antonio told me and poured another shot for me and Carlo. The team we had on call to dispose of bodies came in and wrapped up Emile's men.

"You think he believed your plan of betraying me?"

"I think he was buying it until you got pissed off about Sofia," Carlo said.

"What if that was Sabrina or Janice?"

"We understand, but you can't let your enemy see you sweat," Antonio remarked.

"I need him dead."

"We put a tracer on him, so we'll have his location in a few minutes."

"I'll end this tonight."

"How is your sister doing?" Carlo asked.

"Better." I didn't want to talk about her business, especially with Gael here. Getting him worked up again would only cause us to fight and bicker. He hated that I'd sent her away but understood as my right hand, I needed to make a decision that would benefit the whole family.

"Tonight, you ended Emile Lusting for good." Antonio held his glass up to toast, and I chucked my head and took the shot down my throat, closing my eyes for a brief second to feel the strong liquor pour into my veins.

SOFIA

*S*itting under the lights I was used to doing as an actress, but having to tell my personal business was something I hated. Now I was one of many other celebrities who needed to let the world know how my life changed based on a lie.

"Sofia, thank you for being with us today." Robin Anders from Morning News Life smiled at me, and I thanked her.

"I appreciate you giving me the opportunity."

"Of course, we're all fans of yours here at Morning News."

"Thank you."

"We've had you here many times to talk about your movies and music, but today is different."

I nodded, picked up the glass of water, and took a sip. The audience was gone, and it was just me and Robin sitting together, one on one. She'd been a great reporter for many years. She was respectful with me and understood I wanted to tell my side of things. The media ran any lies they got ahold of, and Cassidy was able to talk them into an exclusive interview.

"Yes, unfortunately."

"You're here because explicit photos and videos were leaked of you and your husband."

"Yes."

"Also, you are currently being accused of murder."

"That's true, but my lawyer is handling that as we speak."

"Tell me what happened."

"My life has been turned upside down by some people who are jealous of me and my family."

"Explain, because there was an explosion at your home."

"Yes, we've been hit from all angles."

"Your husband is not in the business."

"No, he's a businessman."

"He's not here today, correct?"

"No, we thought it would be best if I came alone."

"How did Shamar end up getting killed?"

"Honestly, if I could go back to that day, I would have never left him."

"I know you can't speak about all the details."

"No, because of legal reasons, but I'm innocent, and I want the killers brought to justice."

"The studio states that they're waiting on the investigation before deciding what to do."

"I understand how the business runs."

"Do you remember anyone following you guys?"

I shifted in my seat. I couldn't talk about Mota or Lusting and have more blood spilled, so I lied.

"No."

"What about pictures and photos?"

"Someone planted a camera in our bedroom."

"Was it a fan or a stalker?"

"An investigation is happening right now."

"How are you moving forward?"

"Working with my lawyer to clear everything up and spending time with my children."

"We know you'll bounce back from this, and we hope you'll come back and talk with us again."

"Thank you, and I will for sure."

"I'm Robin Anders from Morning News Life, and you'll find more talk with Sofia Fuertes in an online exclusive." Robin signed off and reached to shake my hand.

"Thank you for being so brave."

"I just want things to get cleared up."

I stood, and we hugged as Cassidy approached me.

"How did it look?" I asked.

"I think you did good. Not too much, but let the audience see your vulnerable side," Cassidy explained.

"Thanks again, Robin." I let the sound guy remove my mic.

She waved and continued talking to her team for the next segment.

"What else is happening?" I walked to the dressing room to remove my makeup.

"Our endorsements aren't happy right now, so we need to handle that."

"I knew it was a matter of time."

"Yeah, they need reassurance."

"Joaquin and me."

"You don't need to say anything. I heard you last night."

I dropped the makeup wipe and turned to look at her.

"You think I was wrong?"

"No, I think you're afraid and have every right to be." Cassidy reached out to hug me.

"I keep having doubts about us."

"That's normal, Sofia, but that man loves you."

"I know, and I love him, but my life is spiraling out of control, and I've never been so emotional."

"You're not pregnant, are you?"

"No."

"Are you sure?"

"Positive." I reached to grab my bag of clothes and walked in the bathroom to change into my sweats.

"The guys are waiting, so we can go back to the house and make calls."

When I stepped out of the bathroom, I placed my hair in a high bun on top of my head and checked to make sure I had everything in my bag. Cassidy opened the door, and I followed her out to meet our bodyguards. We left Times Square and headed home.

* * *

CASSIDY AND I sat in Joaquin's office and made calls to talk about the magazine, clothing, and makeup brands I did business with to convince them nothing had changed. Jianna smiled up at me as I fed her a bottle.

"Sofia, we have a brand to protect," Heather, director of *Fashion Times Magazine*, spoke over the phone. I'd recently done two spreads for them, and it was supposed to come out soon, but Cassidy had received an email that it was on hold pending the current situation.

"Everything will be cleared up soon."

"It's not a good look for us," Heather replied.

"Heather, you've known me for years. This will blow over."

I lifted Jianna and took the bottle out and positioned her over my shoulder when the door opened and Joaquin,

Gael, and Gabriella came in. I waved for Cassidy to mute the call, and I stood to burp Jianna and approach Joaquin.

"I'm on a call. Can you wait outside?" I whispered.

"We need to talk." He rubbed the back of Jianna's head.

I looked down at his clothes.

"What happened to you?"

"That's what we need to talk about."

"Can this wait?"

"I'll take Jianna. Hurry up and finish." Joaquin kissed me on the lips and walked off.

"Cassidy, we have investors, and if anything comes back on us…" Heather complained.

"Heather, either yes or no. I've been a long-time model of your magazine, and I bring in numbers."

"That's not what we—"

I cut her off.

"As the director, you make the decisions, so either the magazine will release as planned, or you'll lose a large demographic." I hung up the phone and plopped down in the chair.

"One down, ten more to go." Cassidy started to call the next person on our list.

"Let me talk to Joaquin first."

"Have you spoken to your lawyer?"

"He should be calling me tomorrow."

"We can hold off if you want."

I stood, wiped the tears away, and composed myself.

"Give me a second, and I'll be back." I left the office, walked to the kitchen, and only saw Martha, JJ, and Madelyn.

"Have you seen Joaquin?" I asked.

"They're in the living room," Martha replied. I bent down to kiss JJ's forehead.

"Mommy, want some!" He held a strawberry out for me to take.

I smiled and kissed his cheek.

"No, baby, you have it. Mommy's full."

"Dinner will be ready soon," Martha said.

"Thanks, Martha."

They continued laughing at JJ, and I went to find Joaquin standing with Jianna in his arms as Gabriella and Gael talked on their phones. I cleared my throat, strolled to Joaquin, and watched the stress in his eyes fade as my hand caressed his cheek.

"How was the interview?" he asked.

I tried to grab Jianna, but he pulled her back.

"She's fine with her poppa." He kissed her on the cheek, and she giggled.

"It was fine."

"We'll have everything fixed soon, my love."

"I trust you."

"Do you?" He lifted my chin and stared into my eyes.

"Yes."

He leaned down to peck my lips.

"We met with Emile today."

"Lusting?"

"Yeah, at Antonio's."

"What happened?"

"He's still alive."

"Joaquin, not in front of Jianna." I covered her ears.

"Baby girl is okay." He snuggled her neck, and she laughed loudly.

"What's the plan?"

"We're going in tonight," Gabriella blurted out.

"Alone?" My brows rose.

"With Carlo and Antonio's men."

"Is that safe?"

Jianna smacked the side of Joaquin's face, and he frowned as she laughed.

"Nothing will keep me from coming home, mi amore."

"So, after tonight, we'll be finished with him."

"I promise, Emile Lusting will no longer bother our family."

"What about Alessandra?" I saw out of the corner of my eye, Gael tensed at my question.

"My father says she's doing fine."

"Maybe it's time she comes home."

"Not now, Sofia."

He pushed Jianna into my arms.

"When are you leaving?"

"After dinner. Stop worrying, and you did good today." Joaquin pressed a kiss on my lips.

"I invited my parents to come for a few days."

"We talked about this already, Sofia."

"With the extra protection surrounding us, my parents are worried."

"I won't argue. When are they coming?"

"In a week."

He rubbed my back and walked me out of the living room with Jianna.

"Call me when dinner is ready," Joaquin said, and I kissed him again before heading back to the office.

BESIDES THE KIDS TALKING, the table was quiet as we ate dinner. Cassidy and Hugo sat together at the end of the table, while I sat next to Joaquin at the head of the family. Martha and Madelyn kept the kids occupied with conversation, but my nerves were all over the place, wondering how tonight would go and if Joaquin should stay home and wait before another attack happened. I pushed the potatoes around on my plate and stared off when I felt his hand caress my palm.

"I don't like it when you worry." Joaquin picked up the napkins and wiped his mouth.

"Hard to mask my feelings about what you're doing tonight."

"I'm protecting our family."

I started to reply and caught myself before raising my voice. The kids never really saw us arguing in front of them, and avoiding glances from his people was one reason I never talked about business out in the open.

"The lawyer should be contacting us soon with updates." Joaquin drank from his glass of water.

"Just be careful."

"Always, sweetheart." He winked, and we continued the conversation about the kids and when my parents would visit. After dinner, we gave the kids a bath and put them to bed. I followed Joaquin outside as he loaded up the car, wearing all black. Cassidy already spoke with Hugo about him leaving tonight and what that meant for them. Joaquin directed his men and then stalked over to me, wrapping his arms around my waist.

"Go to bed."

"I won't be able to sleep until I know you're next to me." I pulled him into a longing kiss.

"Mmmmm…"

"Long as you and the kids are safe, Emile has to pay."

"I understand; I just wish someone else could handle things."

"I'm Ghost for a reason, sweetheart." He kissed my forehead.

I tightened my arms around him.

"Soon as I finish this, we'll be free of him."

"Okay."

"I apologize for bringing this to our home."

"I know."

"Good. Now go inside, and my men will make sure the house is secure." Joaquin released me, and I turned to go back in and shut the front door, watching as he slid down in the front seat and pulled a black skull cap down his face.

"Please be safe." I closed my eyes and sent up a prayer.

JOAQUIN

Gael ended the call and pulled off from the front of the driveway of my home as I checked the bullets in my gun. It was going on midnight, and Antonio's men were ready at every entry point of Emile's stash houses. Carlo texted me the address of Emile and his family near New Jersey. He kept them hidden well from us. He was married with four kids of his own, and I thought they would be in France away from here, but he was bold like me. I never let my enemies see me back down. After making my kids and wife suffer for so long, it was time I gave him payback.

"Carlo has men outside his house." Gael sped up and jumped on the freeway.

"Is the neighborhood crowded?"

Gael passed me the phone, and I saw a text message photo of the home.

"If we do this, it could blow back."

"I want it in the news, show people not to fuck with me."

"Joaquin, as your brother, we need to be clean with this kill."

Twenty minutes late getting off the freeway, he turned down the street of the address texted and saw more cars of our men a few blocks from the home. I slipped the silencer on my gun.

"You can be clean, I want blood."

As soon as he stopped, I jumped out and walked up to Carlo sitting in the van.

"I saw them go in a few hours ago, and he's there."

"He has them in an open area, a plain one-story brick home that we wouldn't suspect."

"Perfect distraction," Carlo said, pushing the door open to hop out.

"I thought you wanted to stay back after the restaurant."

"Janice already yelled at me, might as well get more fun before I'm grounded." He chuckled.

"Same, Sofia didn't want me to leave."

"She'll learn some things we need to do ourselves."

"You ready?" Gael closed in on us.

"I'll take the back, and you cover me, Gael."

"My guys have kids and a woman."

"How many guards?" I questioned.

"Surprisingly, only two."

"He didn't think we'd ever come to his home."

"Which means we need to be careful; there could be traps," Carlo explained, and I agreed.

"Let's go." I looked from my left to right. Checked to make sure most of the homes had their lights out.

"I have a backup plan if we can't take him out," Carlo said.

"What?"

"We call him out."

"It could save us from making a big splash."

"He's inside, probably waiting for us to make a move."

"Did you check the area for any traps?"

"Our men did a check, but that was yesterday. We couldn't get back here until it was dark out."

"Give me his number." I pulled out my cell, and Carlo held up his phone with Emile's number. I glanced up from where we parked and stared at his home that was a few houses down from us as the phone rang.

"Carlo, this isn't the hour to do business," Emile said.

I heard a woman in the background complain.

"This is Joaquin."

The phone went silent.

"I assume you've agreed to my offer."

I gripped the phone.

"To make it easy on you and your family, you should come outside alone."

"I don't know what you're talking about."

"7569 Middletown Ave."

The phone went silent again.

"My family is here."

"Where are you?"

"If you touch them—"

"I suggest you make your way out to me now."

"If you kill—"

I hung the phone up before he could finish and headed toward his home. All the guys stood up with their guns drawn as the door opened. I pulled mine out and held it up, ready to kill him where he stood.

"I'm unarmed," Emile told me.

I motioned for my men to grab him.

"Torch the place."

Emile's eyes rose in shock, and I watched them charge toward the stairs and grab him.

"Wait! My family is inside," he yelled.

Carlo and Gael jogged over to the van as Emile was knocked over the head and pushed inside.

"Tie him up." I started toward the stairs. Carlo stepped in front of me.

"We have him; no need to make any more noise."

"He's right, Joaquin. We don't kill children and women."

I removed the skull cap and ran a hand down my face.

"Think about Sofia."

"The motherfucker wasn't thinking about her when they set that bomb off!" I spat, pushing him away.

"Let's go. We've done enough." Carlo walked off and went to the other van. Gael waited for my call, and I blew out a breath and nodded.

"Leave them."

My heart pounded out of my chest, and rage filled me with leaving behind any witnesses. I would need to put more people in his family for a while and make it seem as though it was a bad deal gone wrong, or he cheated.

* * *

"Arghhh!" Emile screamed as I sliced him on the side of his back. I put him upside down, hanging on chains, and pulled out all my favorite tools that I liked to torture my prey. After I knocked him around a few times, I wanted his death to be slow and painful, the way he slowly tried to kill my family, one by one.

"You tried to kill my wife and children." I pushed the knife against his heart gently, without cutting him.

Blood dripped down his face, stomach, and back.

"I'll leave the country," he muttered slowly.

"Leave the country?" I chuckled, and my men smirked at him trying to buy some time.

I squatted down in front of him.

"I gave you a choice to leave my city alone and my family."

"Please, I'll go and won't be back." He groaned.

"Too late." I held the knife against his arm and sliced up to his armpit.

"Ahhhhh… Mmmmm." He shook, about to go into shock. I splashed him with hot water and burned his skin.

"Give me the gas can." I stood and diced his whole body.

"Fuck you!" Emile shouted.

"Have fun in hell." I flicked the match on him and stood back as he screamed and cried in pain. I smiled and watched my work end. I could now move on and know that he was no longer a threat.

***.

The next day after having breakfast with my family, I had Ezequiel meet me at Antonio's restaurant, now that everything was cleaned up. We parked, and I got out of the car and checked my surroundings. Gabriella stayed out front with Hugo. Gael followed me in, and we spotted Ezequiel laughing with Antonio and Carlo.

"The man of the hour." Ezequiel stood to extend a hand to me.

"Thank you for staying another day."

Everyone sat.

"Drink?" Antonio asked.

"Not today."

Ezequiel leaned forward on the table.

"I take it Mrs. Fuertes is still concerned."

"She is, and I'd like to give her some good news."

The left corner of his lip rose.

"Tell her the case is being dismissed."

"How?"

"We caught one of Emile's men, and he confessed."

"Voluntarily?"

"A little persuasion." Ezequiel chuckled.

"Explain."

"The cops found the car that caused it to go over the embankment."

"The bullets to his head?"

"Traced to Emile's gun ring."

"Is a lawyer on top of everything?"

"Everything should be emailed over, and Captain Herrera is retiring."

"What assurances do we have that it's clearly Mota?"

"Herrera doesn't want any problems with De Luca or anyone else."

"I need a formal statement made to the public clearing her name."

"I'll make that happen."

"For your support, I want to give you a twenty percent stake in Texas."

"Very generous." Ezequiel took a sip of the Hennessy.

"Anything else you might want?" I sat back and made eye contact, letting him know I wouldn't be taken advantage of even if he helped me out.

"I want Emile's stash."

"We have no authority on that," Carlo said.

"There's a reason you gentlemen run New York. I wouldn't think you'd have a problem."

Carlo and I glanced at each other, then Antonio.

"My father might be able to put in a good word," I replied.

He smiled and extended his hand, and I gripped it tightly, leaning forward.

"I appreciate your help, but don't think to try what Emiel has done—"

"Never, my friend."

"Then we understand each other."

"Drinks on me!" Ezequiel held the bottle up in the air.

"The girls want to get together with Sofia," Carlo said.

"Sofia would like that."

"Great, because Janice is driving me crazy."

We chuckled at his statement when a bartender brought a bottle for us with glasses. The rest of the afternoon, we talked more about business and what next jobs I had lined up. I looked at my watch and noted it was almost an hour late. I wanted to get home to have dinner with the family before we prepared for her family to come into town.

"Gentleman, I need to go."

"The wife put you on curfew?" Ezequiel joked.

"That's Janice, not Sofia." I chortled as Carlo glared at me.

"Just remind your wife about the ladies' lunch," Carlo said.

I slapped Carlo on the shoulder and shook hands with Antonio and Ezequiel. I shifted to the exit and put my shades back on to block out the sun. I felt my cell phone vibrate, pulled it out of my pocket, and saw a text from Sofia.

My Heart: Babe, the lawyer called!

Me: What did he say?

My Heart: The charges are dropped.

Me: I told you I'd handle everything.

My Heart: I know, but I figured it'll take a while.

Me: I'm heading home now.

My Heart: I got word from the studio.

Me: What did they say?

My Heart: The film will be released since we filmed ninety-five percent.

Me: I am sorry about your friend.

My Heart: I believe you. See you soon.

Me: Ti amore.

A week later.

"Oh… Joaquin!"

As his tongue brushed against my swollen clit, his hands grabbed my hips, keeping me immobilized. My wetness only intensified as I saw the lust in his eyes for me. After one more swipe of his tongue, he circled his index finger around my core and crawled up my body. Then I grabbed both sides of his face, pressing our foreheads together.

"I never want to be away from you."

Joaquin brushed his lips against mine and released a long-held sigh.

"Forgive me, baby."

"Always." I deepened the kiss, reached between us, and guided his thick member at my opening. He grunted, slamming into me.

"Perfect."

My body was tense, and I felt like I was riding a roller coaster as his shaft hit my spot and pulled back. As his hand wrapped around my waist, I turned on top of him in bed. I took off his shirt, exposing my breasts. When I tipped my head back a bit, I squeezed my legs around his dick, grabbed both hands, and pressed them to my breasts, rocking back and forth.

"You're mine forever, Sofia!" he groaned.

The sweat clung to the sheets as the ringing in my ears and the blurry vision started. I felt my chest rising, ready to climax.

"I'll never leave you!"

Our cries and grunts grew louder. Our lips touched in the middle, our tongues became familiar, and his hands grabbed my ass.

"Right there!" I screamed as my body convulsed, trembling in his arms.

"Shit!" His seed was released, and I prayed we didn't make another baby. I wanted another year before having another child since Jianna was still small.

"Come here." He pushed my wet, sweaty hair away from my face and kissed me on my lips, chin, and nose.

* * *

EARLY THE NEXT MORNING, we were still in bed, and he gripped me around the neck, breathing heavily in my ear as he lifted my leg on the side and slipped his thick member in slowly to play with my clit. I held my hand as he steadily moved in and out of me.

"When are your parents getting here?" he moaned. With my eyes rolled in the back of my head, I gripped his thigh and arched my back a little more, listening to his breathing increase. I felt kisses down my back.

"In about an hour!" I cried out.

"We need to shower and get the kids up." His strokes grew faster, and I pushed back on him to meet his strokes.

My ass slapped against his pelvis, and I felt his nectar run down my legs.

"Joaquin!" I screamed and felt him release a load of his cum.

"You're going to be pregnant soon." He kissed the back of my neck. I pushed him away and sat up to stretch and get out of the bed.

"I have to see what the studio and sponsors will do."

"I do want more kids, Sofia."

"Can we not talk about this right now?"

I went to his side of the bed, kissed him on the lips, and pulled back. He grabbed my arm and pulled me down.

"When?"

"Not right now. We just dealt with a murder charge."

"I'll let you rest for a few months." He grinned, and I rolled my eyes and pushed him back to stand.

"Can you change the sheets!" I yelled from the bathroom.

"Yes, my love."

My parents would be here for a few days, and I planned on making the most of our time together. I wanted to see if Joaquin would be interested in them staying for good. In the shower, I felt strong arms around me, and I jumped in surprise.

"No hanky panky."

"I promise."

"Yeah, right." I stepped up closer to the water and passed him a towel and soap.

Facing him, I washed him across his chest.

"What do you think of my parents moving in with us?"

"Why?"

"I want to take a little time off and spend time with them."

"There won't be any more problems."

"I know, but time is short, and I want to make memories."

"Whatever you need." He wrapped an arm around my shoulder, closing the distance.

"Still not having sex, baby."

He dropped his arms, and I chuckled at the harsh glare across his face. I stood on my tippy toes and kissed him on the mouth and laughed.

* * *

TWO HOURS LATER, my parents sat around the living room with JJ and Jianna, playing with their presents they'd brought them.

"Mom, I didn't think you'd bring this many toys."

She waved me off. "These are my babies; we get to spoil them."

"Are you guys hungry? Martha's in the kitchen making lunch."

"We ate on the plane," Dad replied.

"Where's Joaquin?" Mom asked.

"In his office." I sat on the couch and watched Jianna try to eat the toy doll.

"So tell us how everything is going. The news has been running with lies."

"Everything was a misunderstanding. My lawyer got the charges dismissed."

"Did this have anything to do with Joaquin?" Dad questioned.

"I won't lie, it had to do with some business associates."

"You were caught in the middle?" Dad asked.

"Yeah."

"I'm not happy about this, Sofia."

"I know, but he fixed it and made sure the people who hurt Shamar got what they deserved."

"Your career?"

"I'm going to take some time off."

"For how long?" Mom inquired.

"A few months at least. I need to spend time with the kids."

"I think that's a good idea," Mom responded, lifting JJ in the air.

"What do you think about living with us?"

"Here?"

"It won't be our permanent home, but at least for a few months."

They looked at each other briefly.

"What does Joaquin say?" Dad inquired.

"He's fine with whatever I want."

"If you need us, baby, we're here." Mom stood with JJ and came to sit next to me on the couch.

"Thank you."

"Mommy, look what Poppa got me." JJ showed off the fire truck.

"I see, baby." I rubbed his back.

"What do you have to do today?"

"Nothing, I wanted to see if you want to go shopping."

"How about we pick up some food and have friends come over."

"We can take the kids to the pool out back while Martha gets the groceries."

"You still can't go out?" Dad questioned.

"I can go, but it's safer to keep it under wraps until the news cycle finds a new story."

"That's fine. Come on, JJ." Mom jumped up with JJ in her arms. I laughed at him giggling when she covered his entire face with kisses. Dad followed us with Jianna as she slept in his arms.

"I'll meet you out there. Get Martha a list of what we need."

I headed to the kitchen and saw Martha talking with Madelyn.

"My mom wants to make dinner."

"What do you need?" Martha asked.

"At least enough for fifteen people. I'm going to invite Cassidy and Gael over."

"Sounds fine to me." Martha grabbed the notepad and started taking notes.

Fifteen minutes later, I came outside to the backyard and saw my parents playing with JJ in the pool. Jianna sat on the edge with her feet in the pool.

"Martha's going to grab some groceries."

"Do you need to pick up anything special?"

"We can pick up some clothes at the mall."

"I'll have Cassidy get a personal shopper."

"We're regular people, Sofia. We don't need a personal shopper," Mom fussed.

"I agree, but for right now, just work with me please."

I slipped my sandals off and put my feet in the water. The kids had fun and laughed with their grandparents for about an hour. I stood and helped to take Jianna back in and feed her a new bottle. I stepped into the office to see Joaquin on the phone.

"Let me call you back." Joaquin ended the call and put the phone down.

"I miss you." I went around his desk and placed Jianna in his arms.

"How are your parents?"

"Good, waiting to see you."

"I'm done working. You got me for the rest of the day."

"Martha is back from grabbing groceries."

"You see this?" Joaquin turned his computer toward me, and I read the headlines.

Actress and Singer Sofia Fuertes Found Innocent.

"I know Cassidy probably had back-to-back calls."

"Are you sure you want to take a break?"

"Positive." I slid on top of his desk and crossed my legs.

"What do you think of traveling?"

"Where?"

"To visit my family."

"Does this mean you'll think of allowing Alessandra to come back?"

"Maybe, but not right now."

"I was upset with her, just like you. But you have to forgive her, baby."

"Jianna, tell Mommy you want another sibling." Joaquin coached Jianna, and she dropped her head, laughing.

"No, sir."

"Jianna, move your head if you agree." Joaquin joked, and I smacked my teeth and jumped off his desk to leave him in his office with her.

"Sweetheart!"

"Leave me alone, Joaquin."

CASSIDY

Two days later.

Most of the past few weeks and months kept me super busy with work and less time with Hugo. I knew he was busy with Joaquin, while I was held up handling meetings. The day was going by slowly, and I was headed to lunch with Sofia. We'd just left a final advance screening of the movie she'd done with Shamar. Plus, the girls wanted to catch up, so we said it would be perfect to spend time together and see how the families were doing. I laughed as soon as we walked into Demot's and saw Janice holding a champagne glass in the air, swiveling her hips.

"Please tell me what the occasion is." Sofia stood next to her and planted her hand on her hip.

"Sofia! Finally, you got here." Janice gulped the champagne down.

"What's the champagne for?"

"I'm not pregnant!" Janice announced, and my mouth dropped. Sabrina and Liz laughed at my expression.

"Cassidy, right?" Sabrina waved at me, and I waved back.

"Yes."

"She's my manager now," Sofia said.

"The glow up is nice," Janice replied.

"She's had at least three glasses," Liz complained, taking the bottle out of her hands.

"Hello, ladies. Can I get you anything?" the waitress asked.

"Can I get a glass of water?" I asked.

"You guys don't understand." Janice grabbed a piece of bread.

"Joaquin asked me about another baby," Sofia brought up.

"Hugo and I haven't talked about kids yet."

All eyes looked at me.

"Give it time," all the girls said at the same moment.

"Did Joaquin tell you my husband got shot?" Janice mentioned.

"I thought it was a graze," Sabrina responded and took a sip of her champagne.

"Graze, yeah, right. He thought I didn't have the wound," Janice grumbled.

"I am sorry it got that far." Sofia put her purse on the back of her chair.

"No apology needed; we've been in just as many situations," Sabrina explained.

"Hearing your stories, I'm still surprised I want to marry Hugo."

"We can't tell you not to; we'd be hypocrites." Janice clicked the knife against her glass.

"The situation was crazy, and for Shamar to get in the crossfire…" Sofia closed her eyes and reminisced about Texas.

"We've lost a lot of good people throughout the years," Liz said.

"I'm taking a break from filming and recording," Sofia blurted out.

"How does Joaquin feel about that?" Janice questioned.

"He was surprised but understands."

"You and Hugo." Sabrina pointed at me.

"Unexpected, but I'm happy."

"To be a wife of a soldier takes a lot of strength," Liz said. The waitress came back out and placed our glasses of water down.

"Can we get the pizza and salad?" Sofia ordered.

"Coming right up." The waitress picked up our menus and went back to the kitchen.

"What about going out to the club and celebrating?" Janice suggested.

"The guys won't agree to that," Sofia said.

"Who says they have to know?" Janice winked and sipped on the wine.

"I'm down for a night out."

"If you can handle Hugo's lifestyle, you're fine with us," Sabrina toasted, and I smiled.

"We call ourselves mommy mafia," Janice teased and chortled.

"A full-on text message group," Sofia explained.

"I'm ready for the group chat, but hopefully I can keep my career," I said.

"Just remember what they do keeps them in a head-space you sometimes can't reach," Sabrina explained.

"What do you mean?"

"She means blowjobs go a long way," Janice replied, and I choked on my water.

"She's telling the truth," Liz responded and cut into her tuna casserole.

"Sofia said you girls were funny."

"Welcome to the crew, Cassidy." Sofia raised a glass,

and I joined in as we talked about the kids and going out tonight without the men.

* * *

JANICE SHIFTED her hips in the VIP section of Antonio's club as the DJs played all the old school music from Donna Summer to current Mariah Carey. I laughed when she climbed on top of the table and pretended to be the singer. The guys thought we were having a girls' night in at Sabrina's, and we'd snuck out to the club. I told Hugo I would meet him tomorrow for breakfast, but he insisted on picking me up, so I needed to make sure I was back at her place before the morning.

"Come on, Cassidy!" Janice extended a hand for me to get on top of the table.

"I think you're doing fine without me." I chuckled and watched her flip me off.

"How are your parents?" I asked Sofia.

"Good, watching the kids. I told them we came out tonight."

"You don't think they'll tell the guys?"

"We're surrounded by Antonio's people."

"You guys are boring. Get up and dance," Janice complained.

"How many drinks have you had?"

"Not enough. You guys are bringing my high down." Janice climbed off the table and sat on the couch.

"I guess you thought sneaking out was okay." Hugo stood with Carlo, Antonio, and Joaquin.

"Uhm."

"Baby!" Janice jumped up and held her arms out for Carlo.

All the girls looked at Janice and rolled our eyes.

"I thought you were in charge, Janice?" Sofia questioned.

"She runs her mouth," Carlo teased and grabbed her waist.

"Excuse you, don't give me too much now. That other arm can get a graze too," Janice huffed, crossing her arms over her chest.

I giggled at the two of them.

"None of you told us you'd be here." Antonio walked over to Sabrina and lifted her chin.

"I'm sorry, baby." Sabrina softened and kissed me on the lips.

"I thought the mommy mafia was hard core," I whispered in Sofia's ear.

"They talk a good game," Carlo said.

"Sweetheart…" Joaquin started to approach Sofia.

Janice stepped in front of him, tilting her head to the left.

"The next time you put my husband in the middle of a shootout, think twice," Janice said.

Joaquin held a smirk. "I do apologize, Janice," he said.

"You might be able to get that pretty smile over on Sofia, but I don't play," Janice fussed.

Joaquin looked back at Carlo, and he held his hands up in surrender.

"He has nothing to do with me and you right now." Janice poked him in the chest.

"Janice, you've gotten Sabrina in a lot of mess," Antonio complained.

"Sabrina, remind your husband it's because of me you two even met," Janice spat.

I walked over to Hugo and wrapped my arms around his shoulders.

"I missed you," I said.

"You want to go back to my place?" Hugo wrapped his hands around my waist.

"Love to."

"Cassidy! Cassidy!" Janice yelled my name.

"Huh."

"You give in too quickly, girl."

I chortled and nodded my head.

"I promise to work on that." I winked and turned to grab his hand. We walked out of the club with a few guards beside us. He held the door of his car open, and I slid in and went to open the driver's side and buckled my seatbelt.

"I love you," Hugo said.

"I love you more."

He held my hand up with my engagement ring, and I smiled, leaned over the seat, and grabbed his chin to tongue him down.

"Come on, hurry to your place." I kissed him again.

JOAQUIN

I laughed at JJ as he pushed the plate of vegetables away from him and went for the snack I had on my desk. I'd brought him and Jianna in my office with me while Sofia got dressed for her friend's funeral. Her parents were unpacking and settling in, and I didn't need them thinking I was a terrible father on top of crappy husband. News outlets did enough of trying to break up our marriage.

"Daddy, look at Jianna!" JJ yelled, bringing me out of my daze. I groaned, picking up the napkin to wipe her face and hands free of the chocolate pudding.

"Jianna, you made a big mess on Daddy's desk."

Jianna smiled, and the aggravation left me immediately as her full dimples and piercing eyes filled my heart. I placed her down in the baby seat and helped JJ finish eating when a small knock came to my door.

"Come in!" JJ shouted.

"What are you doing here, JJ?" Sofia grinned to mask her sadness of what today was and approached the desk and kissed the kids.

"Your car out front?" I questioned.

"Yeah, Cassidy is coming with me."

"Are you sure you want to go?"

"I need to go."

"When you come back, we can have dinner with just the two of us." I helped JJ down to play with his toys. I reached out for Sofia and pulled her in my lap, running a hand up her arm. She leaned over and pushed her tongue in my mouth.

"Mmmmm…" She twirled, flicking her tongue.

"When you get back, we can have dinner and dessert." I pulled back and stared into her eyes.

"I'd like that very much."

"Remember, my men will be with you at all times."

"I know, even though everything is done with Lusting."

"Our lives are never simple, sweetheart."

Her hands fell on my chest, and I picked up the back of her hand and kissed her palm.

Sofia stood and rubbed the kids' faces and walked out of my office. I reached for my phone while the kids played.

"I'm surprised to hear from you," Dante said.

"When are you coming into town?" I asked.

"I wasn't planning a trip for a few months."

From Philadelphia, Dante Achille was a friend who like me, was in the business. His family's roots were from Italy.

"Make a trip soon."

"Is this business or pleasure?"

Dante was a trained killer and bastard who no one wanted to do business with. If you owed him, then you were already marked for death. I'd done a few jobs for him that he couldn't reach, and we'd been friendly ever since.

"I hear you're thinking of expanding, and I wanted to make sure of the details."

He chuckled.

"Don't worry, friend. New York is all yours."

"Oh, I'm not worried."

"I'll see what I can do, but business here has ramped up."

"If you find yourself needing to get away, I have a few places."

"I might take you up on that offer."

"Then we have an understanding."

"Clear understanding."

I finished the call, sat back in my seat, and closed my eyes. The next call I needed to make would hopefully make our family whole again. I punched in the number and waited for someone to pick up.

"Fuertes residence."

"How are you?"

"Joaquin!"

"Yes, Mother."

"Oh! I'm so happy to hear from you," Alba said.

"How is the family?"

"Everyone is lovely. Do you want to talk to your father?"

"I spoke with him a few days ago. How is Alessandra?"

"She's adjusting."

"Did Father make her go through with the engagement?"

"No, and thank God he didn't."

I tensed up at her words.

"Why? What happened?"

"I can't say, but I know she's better."

"Should I come out there?"

"We'd love for you, Sofia, and the kids to visit."

"I'll check with Sofia and her schedule. Her parents are here."

"That's lovely. You need family around you."

"Mother."

"No, Joaquin, let Alessandra rest. You've done enough."

"Tell her I'm sorry."

"I will."

"Love you," I said and ended the call.

"Daddy!" JJ squealed, clapping his hands in excitement.

I smiled and went to pick up him and Jianna, and we walked out to the hallway and down toward the kitchen.

"Do you need anything, sir?" Martha asked.

"Did Sofia leave?"

"Yes, about ten minutes ago."

"I'm going to put the kids down for a nap and head out to my office," I explained and turned to head upstairs to their rooms.

* * *

ANTONIO POURED another shot of Hennessy in my glass, and I gulped it down as the monitor on the TV in the bar replayed the funeral of Sofia's friend. The camera panned to her briefly as she hugged his parents.

"I spoke with Dante today."

Carlo and Antonio looked at each other.

"How did that go?" Carlo questioned.

"Normal for us."

"You're both hotheads, so I'm surprised." Antonio stepped around the bar and sat at the end.

"Do you ever think about giving it all up?" I waved my hand around the room.

"This life can never be given up unless it's death," Antonio replied.

"I invited him to visit."

"What are you thinking?"

"He has connections with Russians and the Lusting family."

"Thinking of taking over?" Carlo questioned.

"You don't need the money," Antonio reminded me, and I nodded.

"I would say the same thing to you, but you built clubs and bars all over the world."

"Legit businesses."

My left brow rose in question.

"We can't discuss who is more legit or not," Carlo joked.

"He's right, but I need to make sure I have no more snakes lurking."

"Dante is friendly but deadly if he feels cheated."

"I know."

"How did your night end with Sofia after the club?"

"You mean after your wife tried to put me in my place."

He slapped me on the shoulder and stood.

"Janice is harmless." Carlo walked around the bar and grabbed another Hennessy bottle.

Antonio and I stared at him in disbelief.

"What?"

"Carlo, that woman is nuts," I said.

Carlo flipped me off, and I chuckled.

"Leave my woman out of this," Carlo replied.

"Hugo is next," Antonio mentioned.

"Gael and Hugo," I growled, still not overly happy about my sister being with my best friend.

"You of all people know love can't be stopped." Carlo pointed at my ring finger.

Sofia had our names and wedding date engraved on the inside of the wedding bands.

"I need to get home." I took the last of my shots.

"Where are you off so fast?"

"I promised Sofia a dinner just for the two of us."

"The doting husband," Antonio teased me, and I cursed him out in Italian.

I slid my hand in my pocket, pulled out fifty dollars, and left it on the counter before walking out of the bar to my awaiting car.

"Home?" Gabriella questioned.

"Yeah." My head fell back on the seat and closed my eyes briefly as the soothing alcohol raced through my body. Thirty minutes later, the car arrived at home, and I stepped out clumsily and went to slide my key in the door when it opened automatically, revealing Sofia wearing a long black silk gown. I licked my lips, ready to take her upstairs and undress her down to nothing.

"Wipe that thought out of your head," Sofia said, reaching for her coat.

"Wait, let's go upstairs for a second." I reached for her hand.

She chortled, and I frowned.

"We have dinner plans, Joaquin."

"Dinner will be there. I'll have a hot meal waiting." I licked the left side of her face. She trembled in my hold, and I planted both hands on her hips and squeezed her ass.

"Dinner first and then dessert."

I groaned, pulled back, smirking, and pecked her on the lips.

"I'm going to make you pay."

"Really, how so?"

"You have to wait and see."

"You remember the last time you tried to play this game?"

Sofia tapped me on my nose, and I shook my head, thinking of when I kept her from having an orgasm.

"Sweetheart."

"Dinner first, Mr. Fuertes, and then I might let you have

dessert." She rubbed my chin and walked around me toward the car.

"She drives a hard bargain."

I hopped in next to her and snuggled up close as Gabriella drove us to Demot's for dinner, since it was still early in the night. The kids were fine with her parents, and I had planned on staying at a hotel tonight and never leaving the room unless it was an emergency. She wrapped her hand around mine, and we kissed non-stop as our mouths synced passionately.

I had her favorite foods pre-ordered, so all we'd need to do was sit and have an evening with just the two of us, since I'd rented the entire restaurant for us.

"I like this dress."

"Thank you."

"I'll like it better when you're out of it though." I slipped my hand underneath her strap and caressed the top of her breast. Her breath hitched, and her head tipped onto my shoulder.

"Dinner."

"We will. Afterwards, I have a hotel."

"What about the kids?"

"Your parents are there."

"I know, but I hate to leave them all night."

"They'll be fine."

"All right."

"How are you feeling after today?"

"It was sad, but I'm glad I went."

"Anyone say anything to you?"

"A few photographers tried to get interviews, but I ignored them."

"Long as no one did anything to touch you."

"Everyone knows I belong to Joaquin Fuertes." Sofia put her hand on my chest.

"Have to remind anyone that a problem can become a solution."

"You're a wonderful husband and father."

"The second I put that ring on your finger, I vowed to love you forever."

"You have."

"Even if it hurts?"

She ran a finger across my lips.

"The love pushed through the pain. I will always be yours."

The car pulled up to the restaurant, and Gabriella started to open the door.

"I got it." I climbed out and helped Sofia, wrapping my arm around her, and kept her close. I shook hands with the hostess, and the guard held the door open as we walked through. A banner hung with our names displayed.

"When did you do this?"

SOFIA

The words *Joaquin and Sofia* took me by surprise. My husband wasn't one for the most public displays of affection. For him to rent out a restaurant and show our love in this manner was new, but exciting.

"I had Cassidy help."

"Thank you."

"Come, let's sit down." He headed to the table in the middle of the restaurant and pulled my chair out, and I sat.

"Did the kids get to bed all right?" he asked.

"Yes, my mom gave them a bath and read to them."

The waitress filled our glasses with white wine.

"Thank you."

"Your food will be out shortly," she replied.

"We talked about visiting my family, and I think it's time."

"Okay."

"I want to make amends with Alessandra."

"You should."

"Even Gael has kept his distance unless it's work."

"She's your sister. It hurts, and we all know what that caused."

"At least you still love me."

"That will never change, even when you get into your caveman mode."

"Caveman?" he asked.

"You know that I'm king. I run the house, and you do what I say." I chuckled.

He smirked and shrugged his shoulders. I threw my napkins at him.

"Anyway, I'm happy you're going to make things right."

"When do you go back to work?"

"I'm going to take some time out, but we have the premiere in a week."

"Do you need me there?"

"No, baby, I'd rather not answer questions because all the attention would be gone."

The waitress arrived with plates of baked ziti and baked fish, and we thanked her.

"What do you think of another baby?"

"We have enough with the two we got now," I joked.

"I want another little baby that looks like you."

"Jianna's spoiled enough."

"We can practice at least." He winked his left eye.

"That's the best part."

"How about we leave and get this food to go?"

"Nope, we're going to have a nice dinner as a normal couple." I held my hand up and stopped him from calling the waitress over.

"You've been hanging around Janice too much," he mumbled, and I cackled in disbelief at the frown on his face.

* * *

A WEEK LATER, I pushed the stroller with JJ and Jianna inside through the mall surrounded by five or six guards like I was the First Lady, and they were the Secret Service in their shades. Cassidy and I wanted to pick up a few outfits for the trip that Joaquin had planned for the family. I hadn't seen his parents in so long. This would be interesting since Alessandra and I still hadn't talked.

"What about this dress for Jianna?" Cassidy held up a red and white polka dot dress with matching hat.

"She loves purple." I reached for the other dress in a maroon and purple color.

"Did you have a chance to look at the dresses for the premiere?"

I leaned down to help JJ with the chips in his hand, stood, and continued searching the dress rack.

"I have it picked out."

"We won't need to ask any questions on the red carpet."

"I'd like to avoid that at all costs."

"Already put out a notice that you're not answering anything."

"How are things with you?"

"Hugo and I are good."

"Happy for you, Cassidy. You've come a long way."

"Strange to be getting married, let alone to someone in the mob," she whispered, and I chuckled.

"Just wait until you have kids with them."

"Do we need anything else out here before we head home?"

"No, I think we have enough bags, and the crowd is noticing us."

I looked out the window of Neiman's and saw flashes of light from phones.

"Let me pay for these, and then we can go." Cassidy

took the dress out of my hands and walked to the counter to pay.

Twenty minutes later, we loaded the car up with our bags, and I placed Jianna next to me in the SUV and JJ next to Cassidy as the car drove into traffic. I picked up the doll she was holding and played with it as she laughed.

"You come across as vibrant and fresh in this role," Cassidy read off a headline.

"Love how they try to build you up after tearing you down." I shook my head in annoyance.

"Hollywood for you."

The traffic was light heading back to our home, and we decided to come straight back home after the premiere. As long as I showed my face tonight and did a few interviews online, I should be good to step away from fully promoting.

The car arrived back home twenty minutes later, and I stepped out and carried Jianna inside. Cassidy held onto JJ when the door opened to Madelyn.

"She needs a nap," I told her.

"She looks tired," Madelyn replied, patting her back.

"I have the premiere tonight, and then I'm home for a break."

"Sounds good." Madelyn held out her hand for JJ, and they walked into the playroom.

I sauntered to the kitchen, opened the fridge, and grabbed a bottle of water.

"Hey, baby," Dad said.

He leaned over to give me a hug.

"Hey, Dad."

"Where are you coming from?"

"Shopping with the kids."

"Your mom is outside by the pool."

"I have the premiere tonight. Do you guys want to go?" I asked.

"You know I don't do movie mess." He sat on the chair in front of the island.

"This will be fun."

"Talk to your mother and see if she wants to go."

"Okay, old man. Don't be grumpy when she makes you come." I hugged him from behind, walked down the hall, and saw Joaquin's office door closed.

Shrugging my shoulders, I headed to the back door, pushed it open, and saw my mother and Joaquin talking.

"I thought you'd be in your office." I bent over and kissed him on the lips.

"He's keeping me company."

"How were the kids?" he asked.

"Good for once." I chortled.

"Are they sleeping?" Mom questioned.

"Madelyn has them in the playroom."

"I'll go check on them soon."

"I asked Dad and wanted to see if you wanted to go to my premiere."

"Oh, I'd like that, honey."

"Tell your husband he has to go." I pointed at the house.

"Marriage is a compromise. I see you and Joaquin seem to be doing better."

We looked at each other, and I grinned.

"Better than ever."

"Happy for you, baby."

"Thanks, Mom. So we need to get dressed because we leave in two hours."

"Glam squad doing my makeup?" she questioned.

"Yes, ma'am."

My mom stood, and I grasped her hand and walked

with her back into the house. I saw the team coming in with our attire for tonight, along with hair and makeup.

Mom was right about the compromise in our marriage and being able to show honesty in ourselves. Before, I was at a point of giving this all up, but I knew this man would fight tooth and nail to keep me and our kids protected. I giggled at JJ trying to put his feet in the shoes my dad picked out for his tuxedo. My boy had no clue what would be expected of him when the time came. Would I be ready to let him go out into the world and learn from his father, or would I keep him sheltered from the Fuertes family business?

JOAQUIN

month later.

"Dante, glad you called."

It was therefore suggested that I travel out to Phil-adelphia to meet with Dante, which I agreed to do. Carlo, Gael, and Gabriella would accompany me. The trip back home was still getting worked out once Sofia finished her press tour that had gained considerable notice. A stunning parade of naked women appeared at Achille's club SSO. As I took a closer look, I wasn't interested in meeting him this way, but he wouldn't meet me anywhere else for business.

"We can talk in the back."

The women approached him as he escorted us down the dark hall of his club, and he smiled at them or smacked them on the butt.

"How many have you slept with?" I questioned when he opened the door of his office.

He waved me off and walked toward the bar in the corner.

"Only two this month," Dante replied, pouring a shot of tequila.

"My girl would say your dick might fall off," Carlo joked.

In response, he grunted and held up a glass for each of us.

"How long are you here in my hometown?" Dante questioned.

"I flew in just for today." I unbuckled my coat and relaxed.

"So you want me to broker a deal." Dante came over and sat on the edge of his desk. "Between my connections in New York, Spain, and Italy, we can do big things in Russia."

"I love money."

"The only thing we need to be careful of is blowback from Lusting."

"I heard his people are investigating what happened."

"His wife put out a missing person's report."

"We can make that go away." Dante cocked his head to the right.

"No killing children and women," Carlo said.

"That's the De Luca rules," Dante replied, slid off his desk, and went to take a seat.

"What are the Achille rules?"

"Money and family."

"Our names are too hot right now," I explained.

"So I'll talk to the Russians and Lusting to end the investigation."

"We'll cut you in on the deal."

"Sounds interesting." Dante rubbed his chin, lifting his feet on top of the desk.

"Twenty percent."

"Mota?" Dante inquired.

"Won't be a problem."

"Maybe I should visit New York a little more. I hear your women are exquisite."

"Our women, but you'll have to find your own," Carlo argued, sliding back in the chair.

"We go way back, Joaquin."

"I agree."

"Might get dirty?"

"I'm fine with that, are you?"

He grinned.

"Red is my favorite color." He extended his hand for a shake. I stood and grasped his palm.

"Then we'll do some business."

"You stay and get a dance from my girls."

"We have wives and kids at home," Carlo said.

"Forgot you're on leashes now," he joked, Carlo flipped him off.

"Call me when it's set up," I replied, heading out of his office to the front entrance and our waiting limo.

* * *

Two days later.

Right on schedule, Dante made the connection with the Russians, and Lusting's people were put on warning to keep my family's name out of their mouths. Currently standing at a loading dock to get a shipment of guns from France in crates to unload, Gael and Hugo were with me, and we had the trucks waiting to place everything up to send out to our customers.

"How much are we paying Dante?"

"Twenty percent."

"How many shipments are coming?"

"Two a month."

"We might need to hire more soldiers."

"Have Hugo take over handling the hiring." Hugo looked shocked, but I knew he was loyal. Giving him more responsibly showed that I trusted him outside of taking care of my wife and kids.

"We still need to get someone to replace him."

"He's the only one I trust with Sofia."

"Are you cool with that, Hugo?"

"More than ready," Hugo replied.

"Bigger things are happening." Gael shook his hand.

"Is Cassidy going to be a problem?"

"She's onboard," Hugo answered.

"Then you have my approval and gratitude. When's the wedding?"

"No clue; she's keeping me out of all the planning."

"Reminds me of Sofia."

We watched them pack up the crates and sign off.

"All the women are crazy."

"How's Alessandra?" I asked, and he went silent.

"She wants to come back."

"That's your choice."

"I told her to give it a little more time."

"Whatever you think is best."

"She's special to me," Gael responded.

"The second you have them, never let them go."

"Sofia said you're trying to get her pregnant?"

She'd been acting weird lately, refusing to take a test.

"She wants to wait another year or two."

"What do you want?"

"If it was my choice, she'd be pregnant with twins."

They chuckled as our security of the loading dock signed off and gave me the go ahead to leave. I paid him a hefty amount to keep our stash safe near the waterfront.

"Dante told me how you two met." Gael turned and got inside the driver's side of the car. I climbed in the passenger seat and read over the manifest for the shipment.

"What lie did he tell?"

"He didn't give me all the details and said that's the whole story."

"His life's a book that he refuses to tell."

"Maybe he needs a woman to calm him down."

"We have women; have we calmed down?"

He looked around at the surrounding area, and I chuckled.

"Point taken."

"Exactly: The Fuertes Mafia will never stop."

EPILOGUE: SOFIA

Six months later

The entire house was loud and in an uproar as our families came together to celebrate Jianna's first birthday. Joaquin flew the entire family to Spain to his family's home and hired an event planner to set up the inside and outside with beautiful decorations with Jianna's name across the banner. She was walking now and saying little words that we couldn't understand, but the enjoyment of her learning and growing was something I couldn't wait to see. I'd arranged for Cassidy to hold off on me taking any new film roles, because we planned on staying in Spain for a few months. Even Alessandra was back to her old self and being helpful and supportive. She was staying and getting her design classes transferred, so she could be closer to her parents now that she was pregnant. Gael made it his number-one mission to wait on her hand and foot. Even Joaquin was surprised by how attentive he was being to his sister. The eight hundred thousand-acre land held everything you could need from the main house to a private landing strip. With the kids here, they'd added a little swing set for Jianna and race car area for JJ, which I refused to let him play with since he was too young.

JJ was handsome in the same outfit as his father. I stood on the side, admiring JJ talking with Joaquin's mother. Jianna wobbled behind them to keep up. Her hair was up in little pigtails with ribbons my mother had from when I was a baby.

"Mi amore." His strong hands enveloped my waist, and I sighed, leaning my head on his shoulder. He kissed the side of my neck, squeezing me close.

"She's getting big."

"Mi manchi."

"What are we going to do when they grow up?"

"Have another one." He kissed me on the side of my neck.

I paused and frowned.

"I thought you wanted it to be just us after the kids get older?" I grabbed him around the neck.

He wrapped a hand around my waist, pulling me in close.

"I've thought about that, but something about seeing you with a belly."

"And making the baby doesn't hurt."

JJ ran over to Alessandra and reached for her to pick him up. His parents held on to Jianna, and I laughed at her trying to run away.

"What do you think about renewing our vows?"

"Just us?"

"With the kids, you, and me."

"Whatever you want, sweetheart."

"I guess those nights coming to see me paid off."

"I told you a long time ago, your beauty and voice drew me to you."

"This family has been the strongest when we're together."

"Fuertes is all about family."

"Then let's go home."

* * *

Check out **Aydin a grumpy boss, bodyguard romance** here https://books2read.com/u/mBwaOy .Follow my standalone opposites attract, age gap, military romance **"Exposed"** https://books2read.com/u/bQyYZe . Are you a fan of sports romance? Then download one-night stand, billionaire romance **"Refuel"** https://books2read.com/u/boDyDA. Also, follow it up with workplace, sports romance **"Pressure"** https://books2read.com/u/3Ly1r7 .If you love romantic comedy, fake relationships, enemies to lovers, find it here, **"Something Gained."** Click the link https://books2read.com/u/baGLYy .

Please also check out a second-chance, workplace romance here, **"Heart of Stone Book 4"** https://books2read.com/u/4NXyPG with a host of characters intertwined.

Follow Desiree and Gabriel in *"Temptation"* a standalone contemporary, sports, curvy girl romance. Check it out here https://books2read.com/u/mle1Vv

Check out mafia romance here, *"Antonio and Sabrina Book 1"* https://books2read.com/u/4AxKLo

Any fan of forbidden romance, political? Check out *"**Mutual Agreement**"* https://books2read.com/u/mgzzWX a steamy romance. Pre-order the full novel of "**Nasir**" here click the link here.

Have you checked out **"She's All I Need"** click here https://books2read.com/u/49lkeW a sports, opposites attract romance. What about dark romance that has everything from steamy romance, opposites attract, suspense, thriller, celebrity, and more **"Joaquin Fuertes Book 1"** https://books2read.com/u/mvZlgV

Catch up with favorite characters in this holiday short romance which includes spoilers. https://books2read.com/u/bzd59G

BONUS SCENE: GAEL

"Congrats!" JJ yelled, and I held him up close to Alessandra, so he could kiss the baby's forehead. He was officially four months old today, and I couldn't be happier in life than I was right now. I put JJ back down to run off and play with his toys as Sofia reached for Alexander Gael Velez. We named him with a mixture of both our names, but he looked exactly like me. I was ready to get her pregnant again, but she wanted to wait for when she finished school.

"He looks just like you, Gael," Sofia said.

"I think I helped a little." Alessandra pouted.

Joaquin bent down to hug her, then stood.

"When are you going to make another one?" Alessandra questioned.

Sofia and Joaquin looked at each other.

"We might have something brewing."

"I knew it!" Alessandra excitedly clapped her hands.

"Story will be told later," Joaquin said.

"How did your parents take it about the marriage?"

"They were fine with us eloping."

"How was the delivery?"

"Stressful, and he didn't help." Alessandra pointed at me.

"She was crazy!" I waved my hand in the air.

"Sofia, you had to have seen him. This big, burly mafia guy, running around nervous." Alessandra laughed, and I pursed my lips.

"Ahh, poor baby." Alessandra giggled.

"I get what you mean, Joaquin," I said.

"What?" Sofia and Alessandra spoke at the same time.

"Women hangin' with Janice too long."

They all burst into laughter, but I was serious. Alessandra showed me the text thread for the mommy mafia, and I was disturbed by some of the messages. I even called Carlo to ask if he was safe by living with her because she was nuts.

"Janice isn't that bad," Sofia replied.

"I told Carlo if he needs an alibi, to call me."

Sofia chuckled, and Alessandra got up from the bed.

"We can go out to the patio and eat lunch," she said.

Sofia handed Alexander to Joaquin, and I felt proud to see me and my best friend come to terms and be joined as real brothers and family.

"Maybe you two should create a daddy daycare cartel," Alessandra joked.

"That's enough American TV for you." I pressed a kiss on her lips.

BONUS SCENE: SOFIA

Everyone stood and clapped hands as the happy couple kissed and walked down the aisle. It was a beautiful thing to see Cassidy and Hugo married and in love after denying their feelings for so long. Reminded me a little of myself and Joaquin in the early beginnings and how I'd tried to block out what became a great blessing in my life. The church was full of friends and family on both sides, along with Alessandra, Gael, and the De Luca Cartel. Cassidy wanted to continue managing my career, but I told her it was on hold until she got back from her honeymoon and settled in as a wife. I mean we both found out we were pregnant at the same time, so it was nice to take a break and enjoy life without the headaches of trying to get the latest role or finish an album.

I waved at Alessandra as she held her little boy in her arms. He looked exactly like Gael. His long, auburn hair, icy blue eyes, and chubby cheeks made him look like a doll. I was happy they'd stuck it out and became a family even throughout the hardships we'd endured over the past year.

I gripped JJ's hand, and Joaquin carried Jianna's little feisty butt while I rubbed my small belly in my maid of honor dress.

"Mommy, can we have cake now?" JJ looked up at me, and I smiled. My son was four now and reminded me of his father every day with his dark, bushy brows and how he demanded attention from all the ladies, especially me.

"Not right now, JJ. We have to take pictures and then go to the reception."

"I want cake now," he fussed, crossing his arms and stomping his feet.

"You see your son." I pointed down at JJ, and Joaquin smirked.

"He's fine."

"No, he's spoiled, and it's your fault."

"That reminds of you when I'm devouring you at night," Joaquin whispered in my ear, and I blushed, fanning myself. He put a hand on my lower back and tapped me on my butt.

"I can't believe Hugo is married, and Alessandra and Gael are parents."

"My parents can't either."

"Your father has come around, though."

"Thank Alba for that."

Cassidy and Hugo finished with photos, and the planner directed us toward the limos outside. Joaquin gripped my hand and walked down the stairs with JJ next to him and our parents behind us. Joaquin wanted to rent out Antonio's, but I told him it was too small for the amount of people who'd RSVP'd. We'd rented the Waldorf for two hundred and fifty people, but what made it even more crazy was the amount of cartel families who showed up from De Lucas to Carringtons. It was a who's who of cartel life. The driver shut our limo door, and I helped fasten the kids' seatbelts as we followed Cassidy and Hugo to the reception. Joaquin gripped my hand, moved toward my belly, and rubbed the top before leaning over to kiss me on the lips.

"This is our last one." I pointed at my stomach.

He glared, and I chuckled.

"Mommy, I want a brother," JJ said.

"Well, you'll be happy to know that soon I will find out."

I was only two and a half months along and wanted to keep it a surprise at first, but Joaquin hated surprises, so we decided to find out. While in the States, we decided that living back in Spain for some time would work out best until I was ready to get back into acting and singing. Living in his family's home permanently was not an option, so he bought land and decided to build our own compound on twenty-thousand acres.

"We're here!" JJ yelled excitedly.

"Wait, JJ." I helped him unbuckle his seat. Our son was fast and loved to take off without us, no matter where we went. Joaquin grabbed my hand, helped me step out of the limo, and went to grab Jianna. I walked over to Cassidy talking with the girls and gave her and Hugo a hug.

"How does it feel?" I asked.

"Like I'm somebody's wife." Cassidy giggled and covered her mouth.

"You're a part of the club now," Janice joked.

"As long as she doesn't have to initiate like you two did."

"That comes with the territory," Janice replied and slid her shades down her nose.

"Thank you again, Sofia, for renting out this hotel," Cassidy said.

"My pleasure. Well, Joaquin actually."

"Hugo, let's go inside." Cassidy grasped his hand.

"Only one left is Alessandra and Gael," Janice blurted out.

"I think we'll get an update from them soon."

* * *

Thank you for reading Joaquin and Sofia book 3. If you love dark mafia romance, check out Antonio and Sabrina Struck In Love here.

READING ORDER OF SERIES

Order of Reading
The Early Years-A Prequel Short Story
https://books2read.com/u/49Zjnw
Ruthless Struck In Love Book 1
https://books2read.com/u/4AxKLo
Savage Struck In Love Book 2
https://books2read.com/u/bpED6g
Beast Struck In Love Book 3
https://books2read.com/u/3LpgdJ
Janice and Carlo Captivated By His Love
https://books2read.com/u/b6je6M
Brutal Struck In Love Book 4
https://books2read.com/u/4NQyE9
Joaquin Fuertes-The Fuertes Cartel Book 1
https://books2read.com/u/mvZlgV
Joaquin Fuertes-The Fuertes Cartel Book 2
https://books2read.com/u/4DWwLd
Redemption Struck In Love Book 5
https://books2read.com/u/b5kZ8O

Joaquin Fuertes-The Fuertes Cartel Book 3
https://books2read.com/u/4A5LGp

ORDER OF HEART OF STONE UNIVERSE

Heart of Stone Book 1 Emery and Jackson
https://books2read.com/u/boWPAV
Heart of Stone Book 1.5
https://books2read.com/u/mKELYZ
Heart of Stone Book 2 Jordan and Damon
https://books2read.com/u/ba2OMx
Heart of Stone Book 3.5 Bottoms Up
https://books2read.com/u/4EkjBg
Heart of Stone Book 3 Angela and Brent
https://books2read.com/u/31rx9l
Heart of Stone Book 4 Jessica and Joseph
https://books2read.com/u/4NXyPG

ABOUT THE AUTHOR

Chiquita Dennie is an author of Contemporary, Romantic Suspense, Erotic and Women's Fiction.

Chiquita lives in Los Angeles, CA. Before she started writing contemporary romance, she worked in the entertainment industry on notable TV shows such as *Dr Phil*, *The Tyra Banks show*, *American Idol*, and *Deal or No Deal*. But her favorite job is the one she's now doing: full time writing romance.

A best-selling author and award-winning filmmaker, her first short film, *Invisible*, was released in summer 2017, screened in multiple festivals, and won for Best Short Film. She also hosts a podcast that showcases the latest in Beauty, Business and Community called "Moscato and Tea." Her debut release of *Antonio and Sabrina Struck in Love* has opened a new avenue of writing that she loves.

If you want to know when the next book will come out, please visit her website at http://www.chiquitadennie.com, where you can sign up to receive an email for her next release.

WHAT'S NEXT?

Want to know what happens next?

Follow me on my website to catch the next release.

Reviews are the lifeblood of the publishing world. They're read, appreciated, and needed.

Please consider taking the time to leave a few words on your review platform of choice.

Sign up for updates and sneak peaks at the site below. www.chiquitadennie.com

ACKNOWLEDGMENTS

I want to dedicate this to my team that helps me behind the scenes, from my editors, test readers, graphic designers, and the list goes on. Truly appreciate each of you for keeping me on my toes.

CATALOGUE OF RELEASES

Catalog Releases
    By Chiquita Dennie:
    Temptation
    The Early Years-A Prequel Short Story
    Antonio & Sabrina: Struck in Love, Books 1, 2, 3,4
    Janice & Carlo: Captivated by His Love
    Heart of Stone, Book 1: Emery & Jackson
    Heart of Stone, Book 1.5: Emery & Jackson, A Valentine's Day Short Story
    Heart of Stone, Book 2: Jordan & Damon
    Heart of Stone, Book 3: Angela & Brent
    Heart of Stone, Book 3.5 Jessica & Joseph Bottoms Up
    Joaquin Fuertes (The Fuertes Cartel Book 1)
    Cocky Catcher (A Hero Club Novel)
    Bossy Billionaire (A Hero Club Novel)
    Love Shorts-A Collection of Short Stories

Thank you so much for reading, and if you enjoyed the crazy ride and decide to leave a review, we'd truly appreciate the support.

304 PUBLISHING COMPANY

We showcase authors writing African American, Interracial, Women's Fiction, Urban Romance, Erotic, and Contemporary Romance novels, along with Thriller, Suspense, Poetry, Beauty, and Style Books. Thank you for taking the time out to visit. Join our mailing list to stay updated with new releases and blog posts.